She felt an overwhelming desire to comfort him

Gemma couldn't afford to let herself feel that way about Bart, though. Especially now when he believed she was mercenary.

Instead she asked, "How can I convince you I'm not after your money?"

"Damn the wretched money!" he snapped. "I'm half inclined to give it all away." He looked at her with a penetrating stare. "Would you marry me if I were poor?"

"But that's just what I'm trying to tell you," Gemma shot back triumphantly. "I wouldn't marry you at all!"

When she saw him go terribly still, she added, "I wouldn't marry anybody. I just wouldn't marry. Period."

"Point made," he said coldly. "And I've seen what you do instead...."

Jessica Marchant, a retired English teacher, and her ex-diplomat husband, Peter, have no children but enjoy a wonderful life, traveling extensively. Her first book was drawn from one such journey across Europe. They have lived all over the world, but at present reside in Exeter in Devon.

A Stranger's Glance

Jessica Marchant

Harlequin Books

TORONTO • NEW YORK • LONDON
AMSTERDAM • PARIS • SYDNEY • HAMBURG
STOCKHOLM • ATHENS • TOKYO • MILAN

Original hardcover edition published in 1988
by Mills & Boon Limited

ISBN 0-373-02986-1

Harlequin Romance first edition June 1989

CHAPTER ONE

'YOURS, I believe?'

'Er...well...' Gemma skidded to a halt in the soft sand, shook her dark hair back over her bare, tanned shoulders, and tried to gather her wits.

It wasn't her chase after the laughing two-year-old which had left her so breathless, but the tall stranger who had scooped the child up. Not that he'd noticed the effect he was having. His eyes were all for the little girl, his delight as clear as hers when she chuckled and grabbed his disgraceful old denim cap.

'Thank you.' Gemma took charge of the child, cap and all, and over Jilly's head went on looking up into those dark grey eyes.

In full sunlight, without the cap to shade them, they were more striking than ever. Gemma cuddled Jilly to her skimpy beach-top and felt her own lips curve into an answering smile, though this wasn't at all the kind of attention she was used to attracting with her leggy slenderness and wide hazel eyes. His gaze was gentle, protective, and quite impersonal. He wasn't seeing her as a woman, but as part of the age-old pattern, woman and child drawn close in perfect wholeness.

'She's got a will of her own, hasn't she?'

He patted Jilly's rump and removed his cap from her grasp. To Gemma's surprise he got it without a murmur of protest. Fascinated by him, the child turned in a waft of talcum powder and baby lotion to stare at him again.

'We were only looking for a piece of driftwood, to carry the flag.' Gemma indicated the sandcastle at her feet, where four-year-old Patrick was already flying the scrap of seaweed. 'This little monkey was off the minute my back was turned.'

'It's because she's so full of life. A real Cornish girl.'

'I suppose so. Well—er—thanks.'

Gemma tore her glance away from his and tried to calm herself by looking instead at the sunlit water lapping the rocks below Polruan. It didn't help. The lean stranger, springy hair blowing in the sea wind, seemed stamped on her retina. Under the thick brows, those compelling eyes were the exact colour of a stormy sea, and the strong, high-bridged nose and straight, determined jaw made her think of Cornish granite. Even the shabby jeans and faded blue and white striped sweater disturbed her, clinging as they did to the long, dark-bronzed lines of his body.

Another lithe movement and an unlikely savoury tang drew her eyes back to him. Could that really be celery she was smelling? It was, a head of it sticking out of the duffel bag he had set upright on the sand while he knelt to inspect the fort.

'Is it going to have a moat?'

'I'm just digging one,' Patrick told him. 'You can help if you like, but I've only one spade.'

'What about this one?'

The stranger picked up Jilly's spade. She immediately set up a clamour for it, wriggling to be free of Gemma's confining arms, and Patrick sighed.

'You'd better give her it. She can keep that up for hours.'

'Madam.' The stranger offered the spade with a flourish, the moulded plastic tiny on his big palm, and met Gemma's eyes with a grin. 'I'll just have to dig with my bare hands. Ready, Captain?'

'Ready, sir.' Responding with pleasure to the authority in the deep voice, Patrick picked up his spade.

'Right. You go round that way, I'll go this, and let's see where we meet.'

They set to work while Gemma dealt with Jilly, who always had to do everything Patrick did, and who was now clamouring to join in the digging. Her aunt finally persuaded her to start her own sandcastle with her own bucket and spade, and she seemed absorbed and content, but Gemma still kept a wary eye on her. She wasn't having her running away a second time.

She had often wondered how Tamsin managed to stay so placid while coping with these two young rips. Her sister's patience seemed endless, not only with the children, but with all the washing and mopping and clearing-up they brought. And just now, heavy with her third pregnancy, she radiated a contentment which made Gemma downright envious.

Which was ridiculous. After all, hadn't she enough to be proud of on her own account? Hadn't

she done exactly what she wanted with her life, kept
men right out of it for five years and forged ahead
in an absorbing, satisfying career? So why should
she, just now with Jilly's warm weight in her arms,
have suffered that feeling of regret, of time passing
and chances wasted?

Helping Jilly ease a moulded sandpie out of her
bucket, Gemma decided it must be something to
do with her thirtieth birthday coming up. It seemed
such a settled age, thirty. And she was indeed
settled; she had opted for a career, and stuck to it,
and parted with Kevin because of it. She had made
her choice, and this was no time to start wondering
if she really wanted her future so entirely cut-and-
dried.

'There.' Patrick surveyed with satisfaction the
deep trench round his fort. 'Now we get some water
and fill it.'

The stranger glanced at his large, practical watch,
and stood up. 'Wish I could, Captain, but I've been
too long already.'

As he looked down at them all, Gemma felt the
colour rise in her cheeks. What was it about that
level gaze which did this to her? She too scrambled
to her feet, lifting the indignant Jilly with her.

'Sh!' Glad of the distraction, she calmed the
child. 'We'll go to the water now and you can
paddle. Bring your bucket, Patrick. And,' she ventured another glance upwards into the unnerving
dark grey eyes, 'thanks again.'

The stranger tipped the old cap to the side of his
head. She guessed he meant simply to shade his eyes
again, but his gaze lingering on hers made it into

a special kind of salute. The appreciation in it was warm and gentle; you could almost call it respectful, she realised with a start of surprise. It was so different from the predatory interest she was used to arousing and quelling in the men she met.

It's false pretences, she thought in confusion. He's seeing me exactly the way we all see Tamsin, admiring the kids first, and then me for coping with them so well.

It was the mother he was saluting, not the woman. She wanted to tell him the children weren't hers, yet didn't know how.

If she'd been prepared for him, been able to adopt what she thought of as her 'London' personality, she could have put him right at once. She had met so many men over the years, at parties or in the course of her work as a surveyor for Drew Brothers. It was a game she had long since grown tired of, but she knew exactly how to play it. You kept your ringless left hand where it could be seen, you dropped a hint here and a reference there, and he was soon aware you weren't married and hadn't a regular man in your life. Meanwhile, you would have been receiving the same signals from him, and were ready to consider if you were open to offers.

Mostly she wasn't. Five years ago she had learnt where that led, and once was enough. The fuss Kevin made over her evening appointments to measure or view, the reproachful silences when she went to a business dinner without him, the way she had to break off writing her reports and cook for him when she could have just grabbed an apple and gone on working, all these had convinced her she had no room for a man in her life. And the yawning hours with his friends, the embarrassing evenings with hers when she had been miserably conscious of how often he looked at his watch, all that wasted time had only confirmed her resolve. She had to be alone, had to go her own way and let him—let all men—go theirs.

So why did she feel differently about this one? Why did she long to blurt out that she wasn't married, the children weren't hers? Tongue-tied, she was aware of the smile lingering on them all a moment longer, and then he shouldered his duffel bag.

'My pleasure,' he said, and turned away.

She watched him cross the sand. Readymoney Beach this Saturday morning was full of little family groups enjoying the June sunlight. He padded between the picnics and the deckchairs, intent on some objective that had nothing to do with any of them, and disappeared in the direction of the esplanade.

She supposed he'd be making for the town quay or the yacht club; he had the look of a visiting yachtsman. Gemma hadn't done any cruising herself, but she knew about small boats. During school holidays, helping her father hire them out by the hour, she had acquired an easy comradeship with the owners and crews of the various crafts which used the harbour. Fowey's magical green water and soft air had a special charm for sailing people, who rowed ashore throughout the summer to explore the ancient streets crowded into the steepness of the hill.

'Aren't we going to the sea then, Auntie Jen?' Patrick demanded, and brought Gemma abruptly to herself again.

'Off you go, darling,' she told him. 'I'm coming right after with Jilly.'

But as she held Jilly to kick in the shallows, she realised the stranger was still in her mind, a long shadow between herself and the sun-warmed water. The sight of him loping away with the duffel bag slung over his shoulder had started a shiver in her spine. He was so different from the picnicking groups, so lean and powerful, dangerous almost, like a hunting animal. Yet he had picked up Jilly with such tenderness, entered into Patrick's world so completely, Gemma couldn't help wondering if he had been showing them a side of his nature he normally kept hidden.

Had he children of his own? Somehow she doubted it. That last glimpse of him, hurrying away from the beach with its comfortable family pleasures, told her something about him she couldn't quite pin down. He was ... a loner. That was it, she realised as they trundled the children's water-filled buckets up the beach; he looked like a man who was often alone, who had chosen a life different from the ordinary lives around him.

Just like me, she thought suddenly, then scolded herself and tried to fix her mind on more everyday things. The celery in his duffel bag had probably been asked for by his wife or girlfriend, and he had left in such a hurry because he'd promised to bring it back for lunch.

Finding she didn't like the idea of this tall stranger having either wife or girlfriend, she told herself not to be absurd. She couldn't remember when she had last let a man bother her like this. Yes, she could; it was seven years ago when she had first met Kevin, and look how that had ended.

She stood up. She must distract herself from these uncomfortable ideas, and besides, the children had to be back in good time. Saturday lunch in the cheerful bustle of Tamsin's house, shabby bounced-on furniture and litter of toys and all, was the high point of the week for her parents. They specially loved it when Gemma was there too, so that they had all their family round them again.

Families! Strolling back along the esplanade with Jilly buckled securely into her pushchair and Patrick held tight by the hand, Gemma contemplated hers with good-humoured impatience.

None of them ever gave her the name she had chosen for herself when she first went to London. Sweet-natured Tamsin had tried, and given up apologetically because she 'just couldn't get used to it, Jen.' Their parents, not giving an inch, had declared that there was nothing wrong with the name she'd been christened.

'Jennifer is a fine old Cornish name,' they'd both said, and then went on calling her Jenny, or worse still Jen, just as they always had.

And the entire Roseveare clan thought it high time their Jen settled down. They didn't need to say it, they showed it in every word and gesture. Sometimes Gemma felt their whole way of life was a criticism of her own. Her parents managed to hint in endless different ways that passing exams and belonging to the Royal Institution of Chartered Surveyors weren't everything. Neither was being senior valuer and property sales negotiator at Drew Brothers, though they were proud of her for achieving it.

'But if only,' as her mother frequently sighed, 'if only you'd get married and have a family.'

And dear Tamsin, though she tried to sympathise, couldn't help backing them up. Her very contentment was always there as an example of how a woman ought to be. Look at her now, so pleased to see her children they might have been away for weeks.

Gemma's mother, small and almost white-haired now, but active as ever, unbuckled Jilly and took immediate possession. Then they all moved automatically to the kitchen, where Tamsin reached over the eight-and-a-half-month bulge of Number Three to wipe Patrick's hands and face as if they were precious works of art.

'Has Number Three been kicking?' he asked.

'He did for a while, darling, but he's quiet now. I think he's asleep.'

'Did you enjoy the beach?' Mrs Roseveare asked him, greedy for the attention of both her grandchildren.

'It was great,' he told her. 'We made a fort, and this man helped me dig a moat . . .'

'What man?' Mrs Roseveare looked at Gemma. 'Anybody we know?'

Gemma sighed. Her mother's keen blue eyes, so like Tamsin's, were suddenly interested, and she knew exactly what was going on behind them. Maybe their Jen had found somebody at last, maybe even a sensible hometown boy. Maybe she was finally going to let herself be courted and married, and so get on with the serious business of producing some grandchildren.

Why on earth couldn't she accept that her elder daughter had settled for a career, not marriage? Gemma's irritation was all the worse for the new longings which had been plaguing her recently. Here they were again, and she knew that sooner or later she would have to face and answer the question of what was missing from her life.

But one thing she was sure of—marriage, or anything like it was not for her. She'd made her way this far without a permanent man in her life, and she'd be an idiot to change things now. And, thank goodness, nowadays you could enjoy a man's company without having to marry him, or even live with him. There were lots of other possibilities. She thought, briefly and absurdly, of trying to explain some of them to her mother, but settled instead for putting up the usual smoke-screen.

'You might know him,' she said lightly. 'But I didn't. Jilly ran away, and he fielded her.'

'Honestly, Jen!' Indignant at hearing her grandchild spoken of as if she'd been a cricket ball, Mrs Roseveare clutched Jilly tighter. 'Come in the living-room, children, and see what your grandfather's got for you.' The noise retreated, as if there were twenty grandchildren, and the sunny kitchen was blessedly quiet.

'He was ... an unusual-looking guy.' Gemma ran water over the lettuce in the sink. 'If you saw him, you'd remember.'

'You liked him.' Tamsin made it a statement, not a question.

'Not exactly.' But, even as she denied it, Gemma felt herself relaxing into their old girlhood confidences. 'Only,' she tore up the lettuce, and finished in a rush, 'when I looked at him, I wanted to go on looking.'

Tamsin put down the oven-cloth and checked over a mental register of people she knew. 'Local?'

'I shouldn't think so. A yachtsman, more likely.'

'Oh.' Head on one side, Tamsin registered these few scraps of information and added some of her own, 'Raggy old sweater and jeans, terrible hat? Very sunburnt?'

Gemma nodded. 'And fairish hair, a bit too long...'

She paused, baffled. What was it about the stranger which had made such an impression on her? He wasn't handsome, his nose was too beaky and his eyebrows too thick. Was it those storm-grey eyes, the eyes of a man who knew how to get what he wanted? Or was it the wide mouth with its special, warm smile for her and for the children he thought were hers?

'I know who it was,' Tamsin said. 'That was Bart Rule.'

Gemma blinked. 'In Fowey?'

'Why not? He was born in St Austell.'

'But he hasn't any ties here now.'

'Maybe he just wanted to see the old place again.'

'I suppose so,' Gemma agreed reluctantly.

Somehow it didn't seem Hobart Rule's way, to be going over old ground. His clay-worker father had died young, his mother just as he finished school, and news of him nowadays came mostly from the papers. The rest of the world knew him as the controller of a computer empire and difficult husband of a glamorous television star. Here in his home neighbourhood he was still Bart, as he'd been in his boyhood, and they all took an interest in his doings, but nobody had seen him here for twenty years.

People enjoyed talking about him, though, and he gave them plenty to talk about. Apart from the reports of takeover bids and huge donations to charity, he was often shown attending a first night or an influential party. He turned up on television quite often too, and only recently had publicly fallen out with a press photographer in a fashionable bar.

Casting her mind over these various images, Gemma saw why she'd failed to recognise him. He was never pictured in anything but elegant leisurewear or perfectly cut suits.

'What about those clothes, then?' she demanded.

'He's on holiday,' Tamsin pointed out. Herself stunningly beautiful in a pair of jeans done up with elastic and one of her husband's old shirts, she clearly felt that no other explanation was needed. Of course you didn't dress up unless you had to.

'He's moored in Wiseman's Creek, on a boat called the *Felicity*,' she went on helpfully, and finished with a sideways glance, 'alone.'

'Oh?' Gemma turned the lettuce leaves under the tap, glad of the noise of running water to cover whatever her voice might be giving away.

'You read about his divorce?'

Gemma nodded, letting a curtain of dark hair fall over her face. A year ago, the papers had been full of Caroline Lang's divorce from Hobart Rule, though none of the reasons they had given seemed more than mere guessing.

'She's gone to America.' Tamsin's brow wrinkled as she tried to recall the details. America for her was as distant and exotic as the moon. 'To make films, I think. There didn't seem to be another man.'

'Or woman?' Gemma tried to keep her voice casual.

'Bart Rule's marriage would never break up over another woman,' Tamsin said decidedly. 'As long as he was married, he'd never even think about other women.'

'However do you know that?'

'Well, Mrs Vosper at the corner... You can laugh,' Tamsin broke off as she observed her sister's smile, 'but Bart Rule's still one of ours. We know him.'

'Including how he runs his love-life?'

'All the time he was here, he always stayed with the one girl,' Tamsin insisted, 'Sally Kivell it was, that married Mrs Vosper's nephew.'

'So he has to be a one-girl man?'

'Well, it was Sally who finished it, because of him going away. He took it hard.'

'Or so Sally would like us to think,' Gemma teased gently.

'Jen, you're so...so cynical these days!'

'Sorry.' Gemma shook out the last lettuce leaf and turned off the tap. 'Go on about Bart Rule.'

'Where was I? Oh, yes, why he's here alone. I reckon he's trying to get over a broken heart.'

'Honestly, Tam!' Gemma couldn't help laughing aloud this time.

'I don't know why that's so funny,' Tamsin exclaimed, heated at last. 'He was married for five years—isn't that a big enough part of anybody's life?'

'Sorry, love. It's only...I don't know when I last heard anybody talk about a broken heart.'

'Doesn't mean people don't have them,' Tamsin replied with spirit. 'Why else would he let go of Rule Electronics?'

'Has he?'

Gemma was startled in spite of herself. As the name implied, Rule Electronics was Bart Rule's great achievement in life. He had built up the conglomerate from its earliest beginnings, and he was still only in his late thirties. Surely he wouldn't be selling his controlling interest so young?

'So the papers say,' Tamsin assured her.

Gemma smiled again. 'That could mean anything.'

'Suit yourself,' Tamsin passed over a cloth for the lettuce. '*You* think of a reason for his being moored in Wiseman's Creek, miles from anybody, then. And getting cross when he's recognised.'

'He always gets cross with the gossip columnists.'

'I'm not talking about gossip columnists, I'm talking about old schoolfriends.'

Gemma nodded. She could see how the town would be intrigued by the mystery of this visitor who had grown up here but would rather be treated as a stranger. She was intrigued herself.

More than intrigued, she admitted as the afternoon wore on. She knew it wasn't just his looks which kept him in her memory like this, yet there he lingered, smiling down on her, smiling down on the children...

That was it. She didn't understand it yet, but the key was there somewhere. The children had brought them together, Tamsin's children who might have been hers, and that had given her a...a feeling about him. A feeling that this chance encounter was somehow important to her, had presented her with an opportunity she mustn't throw away.

For the moment, Gemma didn't bother to analyse her ideas any further than that. She had always been a woman of action, used to carrying out her decisions as soon as she'd made them. Now, she decided to make sure she met Bart Rule again before her weekend was over.

Sleepless that night in her old white-painted room, she wondered how she could work it. Should she start by taking Jilly and Patrick into town again tomorrow morning, for instance, and look out for him there? He was the kind of man you noticed from a long way off, and if he was anywhere in sight she wouldn't miss him. What she would do then she didn't know, but she'd think of something.

And if she didn't see him in the morning, what about taking out a rowing-boat in the afternoon? She often did that on Sundays when she was at home, pottering about the harbour, visiting old haunts like Wiseman's Creek, chatting with any yachtsmen who were moored there.

After all, she and Bart Rule had a lot in common. What could be more natural than a meeting between two locals who had each left town and made good in their own way?

As it turned out, she might just as well have forgotten her schemes and concentrated on getting some sleep. Next morning, young Tim Rowse delivered the Sunday papers, agog with how, last night, a local cameraman and reporter had hired his father's boat. Tim himself had taken them out in it, to Wiseman's Creek, to try and interview Bart Rule. They'd caught him having his supper, and he hadn't uttered a word.

'Not a single word,' Tim assured them. 'Just upped anchor and away. Nearly rammed me, he did.'

The newsman had wanted Tim to follow, but his little seagull engine couldn't compete with the *Felicity*'s great inboard diesel, and he had left them behind with ease in the narrows of the harbour. By the time they had toiled out to sea, he had hoisted sail, and their last view had been of the *Felicity* speeding away with sails spread wide, east round Pencarrow Head.

'Making for Looe, I suppose,' Tim had commented. 'He wouldn't get much further by daylight in that old tub.'

'You don't mean the *Felicity*?' Gemma asked in surprise.

'Well, not so old maybe, in fact she's probably new. But she certainly is broad in the beam.'

Gemma remembered Tim's ambition to own a racing yacht. 'Not what you'd buy yourself, then?'

'That fibreglass bathtub?' Tim exclaimed in disgust. 'Not likely. That's a married man's boat, with room for all the kids.'

'Nothing wrong with being a married man, Tim Rowse,' Mrs Roseveare told him tartly, 'as you'll find out one of these days.'

'Still, I see what Tim means,' Gemma said. 'You'd expect Bart Rule to be sailing something faster, wouldn't you?'

She had to say something, to keep the talk going and to cover her annoyance and frustration. Why couldn't the newshounds leave people in peace? She couldn't go chasing Bart Rule to Looe or wherever he'd gone now.

She spent the rest of Sunday trying to put him out of her mind, trying to control the blank emptiness which descended on her whenever she let it, but she couldn't hold it back entirely. When she boarded the train to London, the blankness settled heavily on her spirit, and seemed to weigh her down more with every turn of the wheels that sped her away from home, her home and his.

CHAPTER TWO

'IN CONCLUSION,' Gemma dictated into the microphone, 'I have no hesitation in recommending this property as good value at the price being offered for it.'

Which was hardly surprising, seeing the offer had been made on her advice. She had surveyed this place before she went to Cornwall, and found it in good repair, except for a little woodworm under the stairs which would need to be treated.

'Can you do the usual covering letter, Sarah?' she went on into the microphone. The phone rang, and she reached for it as she added into the recorder, 'I'd like this report to make today's post if possible, please.'

'Hi, Gem.'

'Oh. Hello, Kevin.'

She settled back in her swivel chair with a sigh for the way time went. Seven years ago this light, relaxed voice would have sent her into raptures. And two years after, when she'd just left him, it would instantly have put her on her guard. It made her feel very old, talking to him like this without the least overtone of affection or reproach.

They still met now and again at parties, but not often. Once they had gone their separate ways, it was glaringly clear how little they had in common, and they moved in completely different worlds. Last year he'd invited her to his wedding, and she had sent a pair of salad servers, but on the happy day was otherwise engaged.

'How's Lynn?' she asked politely.

'Blooming,' came back down the line with great enthusiasm. 'That's why I'm calling, really. We need somewhere bigger.'

'Another flat, or a house?' She sketched a triangle on her scribbling block.

'A house this time. Lynn wants a garden, for the baby.'

'A baby?' She put a square below the triangle. 'Great!'

'He's not due for months, but we're thrilled.'

Gemma thought of Tamsin, placid and tender above her eight-months' bulge. For some reason she was glad Kevin couldn't see her as she drew little legs on the square, and softened the triangle with curved shading. She went on doodling while she listened and made notes about the house Kevin wanted.

'Well, we'll do our best,' she said when he'd finished. 'We ought to get an excellent price for your present place.'

'It's pretty central,' he agreed, 'and I believe one-bedroom flats are in demand just now.'

She laughed. 'Everything's in demand. You know London.'

'Don't I! I'm trying to persuade the bank they need me in a provincial branch.'

'But wouldn't that mean less interesting work?'

'Not at all, only different. What about you, Gem? Why are you still hanging on here?'

'You make me feel like a forgotten overcoat.'

Gemma managed another laugh through her irritation, and kept her eyes on the treetops outside the window of her second-floor office. She loved the play of light and shade in that foliage, the blackbirds and sparrows coming and going among the branches. That was one of the reasons Kevin had given for his belief that she was a country girl at heart, a belief she resisted all the more because she was half convinced he was right.

Here he went again. 'Have you thought any more about setting up for yourself outside London?'

'Oh, one of these days.'

'In Cornwall, maybe,' he prattled on. 'At least you'd be home, even if you only want a career.'

'Less of the only!' Telling herself he was a customer, she tried to keep her voice light.

'Oh, I know you've always thought your career important. And you've still plenty of time, really.'

Gemma gritted her teeth. The way he said that word 'really' made her feel the weight of every one of her thirty years.

'Lots of older women have families,' he was blundering on. 'Look at my mother.'

Who had always insisted grimly that in her day a decent woman waited to be married before she lived with a man. And who never concealed her impatience to be knitting tiny garments. In the opinion of Kevin's mother, the only worthwhile work for a woman was producing children.

Gemma suspected Kevin thought so, too. He'd fought her career for two years with every silent weapon in his armoury. She should have seen from

the start what he was really looking for, the kind
of woman his mother had trained him to expect.

And that, she supposed, was what he now had.
With his Lynn, and a baby on the way, even his
mother must be satisfied. In fact, it had all come
right in the end, and each of them now had what
was best for them. Hadn't they?

'I expect your mother's very happy with your
news. Now,' she went on quickly before he could
get going again, 'do I take it you're giving us sole
agency?'

She made an appointment to measure and assess,
and hung up, resolved to let one of her juniors do
it.

Poor Kevin, no wonder she'd decided she could
live without him. Trying to remember why she'd
ever fallen for him, she found quite a different man
forcing his way into her mind. She screwed up her
eyes and shook her head, but he wouldn't go away.
Still needing to escape those heavy-browed, storm-
coloured eyes alight with a tenderness all the more
striking for its underlying strength, she glanced at
her watch.

No wonder she couldn't think straight. She hadn't
stopped since nine, taking her lunch time apple and
black coffee here at her desk. Rising for her long
overdue break in Kensington Gardens, she took her
handbag and made for the cloakroom.

In this white room, the June sunlight was par-
ticularly cruel. Shrugging into the moss-coloured
silk jacket which brought out the green in her eyes,
she paused for a glance into the washbasin mirror.
She reckoned to do a good job on her make-up in

the morning and then forget it, and sure enough it was still in order. But now it only seemed to emphasise the permanently tired skin under her eyes, the lines starting to ray upwards from them.

Damn Kevin, she wasn't going to let him make her feel a hag. With a deliberate effort she squared up to the glass for a long, cool appraisal. Her skin was still good, its normal creaminess flushed now with Cornish sunshine. She always knotted her dark hair to the back of her head for work, but as usual it was straining to be released, the cloud of little tendrils about her brow and cheeks softening the firm oval of her face. Her eyes might be a peculiar mixture of brown and green, but they were at least candid-looking in their wide hollows, and her full mouth had been described as generous.

Only it wasn't generous at all; it was too held-in and pursed-up for that. And those eyes might be clear and well-set, but weren't they just a bit...calculating? More than a bit, if she was honest. At the moment they looked downright hard, just as her carefully dieted slenderness looked merely...*starved*.

To hell with it, Gemma thought. As she swung down the stairs her face was vibrantly alive, her walk smooth and strong as a young cat's, but she was quite unaware of the improvement. She had no idea why the postman on the front steps halted his letter-sorting to stare at her.

'Who's the lucky feller today? Peter Pan?'

She flashed him a grin, and joined in his joke about her daily exercise. 'I thought I might give Prince Albert a whirl.'

'Mind he behaves himself.'

'Sure thing,' she responded, and felt much better as she went on her way. Perhaps she wasn't right over the hill yet.

The Gardens smelt as they always did after a shower, of dogs and traffic fumes. Still, the shrubs and grass and trees were green, and the sharp scent of newly turned earth reached her from a flower-bed where canna lilies were being put in for the summer. She kept up the long strides she so much needed after the hours at her desk, and the gilded spire of the Albert Memorial guided her to its statue-laden plinth.

Today a school party was swarming over it. She smiled at the children's fascination with the grand marble groups, all elephants and buffaloes and noble savages, which were meant to show the four pillars of Victoria's empire. But when a young woman made her careful way through the crush, Gemma looked quickly away. Yet it was a common enough sight, a woman with a baby strapped close.

She usually went back by the Round Pond, but today she took a different path. This June afternoon was bound to bring out the nannies with their charges, and for some reason she didn't want to see babies in prams, or toddlers playing.

As it turned out, the way she did choose was no better. Crossing the bridge over the Serpentine, she came to a stop with her heart jumping and her blood hammering. A lean figure was ambling towards her, tanned and lanky in striped jersey and jeans, bare feet thrust into canvas shoes. He came nearer, pulling off a disgraceful old cotton cap in mock-courteous greeting.

To show crew-cut dark hair, and dark eyes that returned her interest with some to spare.

'Er...sorry.' she gave him a weakly apologetic smile. 'I thought you were someone I knew.'

'As of now, I am,' he answered promptly, and went on with American resourcefulness to give her his name.

'I...I must go,' she said as he waited for her response. 'Er... Sorry again.'

She hurried on, cursing herself. This man was very young, young enough to wear funny clothes for the hell of it, and certainly years younger than she was. Besides, did she really expect to see Bart Rule in his sailing gear, here in Kensington Gardens? In town he would wear the best suits Savile Row could tailor, and he probably never walked in the park anyway.

What a pity she hadn't managed to see him again yesterday as she'd meant to. She might have found out by now that he was an ordinary human being, after all. Instead, she'd known nothing but this wretched feeling of flat emptiness, all through her journey back to London, right into her St John's Wood flat.

This was the place she'd bought after she'd disentangled her affairs from Kevin's. It was costing her more in mortgage than she liked to think about, but it was worth every penny to be somewhere she could organise exactly as she pleased. Usually it gave her a kick just to turn the key in the lock, and never more so than after a weekend with her family.

So why, last night when she arrived back in it, had it suddenly seemed so...so *sterile*? Why had she skipped all the routine chores which usually prepared her for Monday? The measuring-out of her breakfast muesli, the writing of instructions to the two enterprising young men who came in and cleaned, the jotting of items for her shopping list, all had seemed a tedious waste of time. She hadn't even unpacked, only dumped her hold-all in her beloved frilly bedroom and slumped in front of the television, not knowing what she was watching. Then she'd gone to bed, and dreamed things she would rather not think about.

But she had to think about them, hadn't she? This episode in the park showed how firmly Bart Rule was lodged in her mind. All morning, however determined she had been to settle down to the job she enjoyed so much, she had found pictures forming unbidden before her inward eye. Over and over, dark-bronzed feet had straddled the sand in old canvas shoes, powerful hands had scooped little Jilly up into the sunlight, storm-grey eyes had laughed back at the laughing child.

Several times since she'd left Kevin she had been haunted like this by some man who attracted her. Each time, she had got to know him better and he had ceased to be interesting, sometimes become downright dislikeable. Very well, then. Now was the time, with no telephone to worry her and the vigorous rhythm of her walk sharpening her mind, to work out a way of meeting Bart Rule.

Scraps of her chat with Tamsin floated back to her. He'd been divorced last year. And there were those rumours about Rule Electronics changing hands. Maybe Bart Rule was altering his way of life. And if so, he'd have a house or a flat to dispose of.

It didn't matter whether he wanted to sell or rent, she could be equally useful to him either way, and it gave her a perfect reason to ring his office. He was probably still on the *Felicity*, but she could ask his personal assistant or secretary or whatever for an appointment to speak with him personally. If she turned out to be right about his needing an estate agent, then she had the full weight of the long-established firm of Drew Brothers to offer. And if she was wrong, nobody would blame her for trying.

Either way, she'd have met Bart Rule. She clattered up the stairs to her office, relieved to have come to a decision, more at peace with herself than she had been since that disquieting Saturday morning at Readymoney Beach. She'd see to it right away, get on the phone at once and have the rest of her day to think about something more useful.

The telephonist at Rule Electronics informed her that Mr Rule had both a personal assistant *and* a secretary. What was more, the personal assistant Mr Derby had a secretary too, and anyone who wanted to talk to Mr Rule had to start there.

'Shall I put you through?'

'Please,' Gemma said, and found herself explaining her mission to another cool female voice.

'I'll see what Mr Derby thinks, and ring you back.'

In fact, it was Mr Derby who rang back. 'You understand, I'm sure, how valuable Mr Rule's time is,' he explained smoothly. 'If you care to come and see me, I'll put in a memorandum. Then it'll be up to him.'

'So I'm to be vetted,' Gemma thought, and controlled her impatience. A man had a right to his privacy, and if it took four dragons to guard it, then that was what it took. She was at least finding her way into the Rule empire; the next thing was to make out as good a case as possible to its inner circle. Adding further shading and lines to the ever more complicated figure on her jotter, she accepted an appointment for five.

That left her two hours to work through her in-tray. She took out the next letter, from the client whose flat wasn't selling, and set herself to tell him as tactfully as possible that he was keeping the price too high. Then she had to check who would be free to measure Kevin's flat, and choose leaflets of houses which might interest him and Lynn. After that she just had time to edit the report the typist had put into the word processor, and give instructions for the final printout to be left on her desk; she would return this evening to sign and post it. Then she could drop her pens into their tray, put away her cassette, and lock up her filing cabinet in her usual methodical manner.

Part of the clearing-up routine was to check over her jotter. She tore off the top sheet and studied it as usual, making sure all her scribbled notes had been dealt with or stored somewhere more permanent. She was about to crumple it for the waste-

paper basket when today's doodle caught her eye,
and she blinked. The triangle, the square, the little
legs, the shading, all had come together now as a
picture—but of what?

She could hardly believe it, though it was clear
enough. During the afternoon she had added fluted
edges to the shading, and solid arcs under the legs,
and now she had a complete, detailed picture of an
old-fashioned, frill-draped cradle.

'Let's face it, Jen,' she murmured to herself, very
Cornish in her surprise, 'you're broody.'

She meant to crumple the paper up, but found
she couldn't—it would have felt like sheer cruelty
to something small and defenceless. Exasperated
with herself, she folded it and slipped it into the
pocket of her full-skirted dress.

It was exactly five o'clock when she presented
herself on floor nine of the Rule building. Mr
Derby's secretary, cool as her telephone voice, an-
nounced Gemma on the intercom, and Mr Derby
answered from the connecting room that she was
to come straight in. He made Gemma think of a
sparrow, round and brown and aggressive, but he
listened carefully to her account of the services
Drew Brothers could offer.

'I'll make my report, of course,' he said at last.
'It's only fair to tell you though, that Rule
Holdings...' He broke off as the outer door of his
office shot open.

Gemma swallowed hard as a lean, tall figure
strode in from the secretary's office. She was
looking up into the same storm-grey, heavy-browed
eyes which had been haunting her for two days.

He wasn't after all in a suit, but a striped, turtle-necked T-shirt and jeans which were a newer version of Saturday's rags, as if he wore his clothes to shreds and wouldn't part with them. Over those, a beige-lined shirt-jacket in a subtle shade of green-blue-grey swung open, but could be buttoned to its beige collar to keep out the wind. So he still looked as if he had come ashore from a small boat, especially with the lengthways-zipped duffel bag he was swinging down from his shoulder.

'Hi, Bart.' Mr Derby was giving him a resigned look. 'So it didn't work?'

'The boat worked a treat,' Hobart Rule growled as he thumped the duffel bag to the carpet.

'And that's why you're back a week early, without a word of warning.'

'You know damn well why I'm back, Jim.'

'I'm not saying it!' Mr Derby held up his hands in a mock-soothing gesture.

'Doesn't stop it being true. You told me so, didn't you?'

'So I did. Well, fancy that!'

Gemma blinked at the ironic exchange. Did the head of Rule Electronics really let his employees talk so freely, even when he was in this black a mood? It seemed he did; the older man was looking at him now with an exasperated affection so much a part of their relationship that Bart Rule was taking it for granted.

'I'll tell you all about it later,' he snapped, and turned to Gemma. 'Hello.' The furrow between his brows smoothed. 'What are you doing here?'

'You r-remember me, then?' Now she was facing him at last, she found her mouth had gone dry.

'Readymoney Beach,' he confirmed. 'Last Saturday.'

A sharp pain in her palms made her realise she was digging her nails into them. She deliberately loosened her hands and took a deep, steadying breath. His frown when he first appeared had been thunderous, but he was smiling now with no trace of his earlier temper, so why was she more nervous than ever?

'How are the kids?' His voice cut into her chaotic thoughts.

She remembered then that he still thought she was their mother. She'd have to sort that out, yet she was reluctant to begin. It was so good to have him smiling at her like this, to see the bleak, hard face light up with gentle interest and to bask in its sudden warmth. The idea slipped unbidden into her head that this man would always look after his own.

'Th-they're fine, thank you.' she stammered. 'But, er...'

'Bart,' Mr Derby stepped in swiftly, 'this is Gemma Roseveare, who thinks she might be useful to you over Greatwoods.'

'She does?' He scrutinised her. 'In what way?'

'I'm chief surveyor for Drew Brothers, Mr Rule.' Gemma was relieved to find her confidence returning as she pronounced the status she had worked so hard to achieve.

'Drew Brothers,' the frown was back between the heavy brows, and his voice held a new hardness, 'the house agents?'

'Estate agents,' she corrected him crisply.

'What is all this?' He turned to Mr Derby. 'How do they get on to these things? I've hardly thought it through, and here they are like vultures...'

'Vultures!' Gemma felt the heat flame in her cheeks. 'I resent that, Mr Rule.'

He murmured something under his breath which sounded exactly like the things her father said to relieve his feelings at some small mishap. When he spoke again his voice showed irritation banked down and ready to flare, but it seemed mostly with himself.

'I'm sorry, Mrs...Roseveare, wasn't it? Nothing personal.'

She nodded stiffly, feeling uncomfortably in the wrong. She had, after all, acted on a hunch, from rumours; maybe she'd been, well, pushy. Then she straightened her shoulders; she was here to do a job and she was going to get on with it.

'Yes, I'm called Roseveare, Mr Rule, but...'

'A Cornish name.' He seemed glad to be reminded of their first meeting. 'Did you marry a Cornishman?'

She decided that this was not the time to say she hadn't married anybody. It would only carry them further from the point.

'I was born in Fowey,' she told him briefly. 'Now...'

'How could you bear to leave?'

She shrugged. 'For the same reason you did, I expect.' I had a living to earn, she would have gone on, but he didn't let her.

'Unless Fowey's changed, you'll have heard why I went.'

She blinked at the explosive tone, and deliberately kept her own voice even and cool. 'Last Saturday, you mean?'

'The damned Press got on to me, didn't they?'

'I heard about that, yes. It would only have been a——' she paused, choosing her words '—a paragraph in the local paper.'

'Only?' he repeated with suppressed fury. 'I see you've no experience of these things.'

She bit her lip, determined not to respond to the angry tone. 'No, I haven't.'

'The local rag would have been just the start of it. After that...' He put a hand to his eyes as if fatigue had suddenly caught up with him. When he took it away, his face was drawn and sad. 'I'm sick of finding lies about myself in the papers.'

She was silent, remembering how his marriage to a television personality, and its break-up, had been raked over endlessly for months.

'Right,' he went on, distant and formal. 'So you'd like to handle Greatwoods for me?'

She nodded, glad to be back to business. 'Which is it to be, letting or selling?' Until now she hadn't known Greatwoods existed, but whatever it was, she knew she could deal with it.

'Selling. And there'll be a flat in Belgravia too, for letting. I'm getting rid of everything.'

'So that's that,' Mr Derby burst out in obvious distress. 'You might have told us, Bart.'

Bart Rule dropped his voice wearily. 'I've only just decided, Jim. And you know I'll see you all right, you and everybody.'

'It'll mean changes.' Mr Derby closed his mouth tight, then sighed. 'Oh, well, it had to come. Was it anything that happened on the trip?'

'You know, I think it was.' Bart Rule was studying Gemma again with grim resignation. 'I think perhaps it was. Look,' he consulted his watch, 'I could see Mrs Roseveare while you're finishing here.'

'Why not?' the other man indicated the leather-bound engagement book on his desk. 'You're still officially away, so you haven't anywhere else to be.'

'Nowhere,' Bart Rule agreed bleakly. 'Have you time for a drink with me before you catch your train?'

Mr Derby opened his blotter on a pile of letters for signing, and reached for his pen. 'If you want to talk, Bart,' his dark eyes were full of something which now looked very like compassion, 'I'll catch a later one.'

'Thanks, Jim.'

Bart Rule opened the door of his inner office and nodded Gemma in. Clutching her briefcase, she walked by him, then stiffened in shock as her arm brushed his. What was this tingling which transmitted itself through several layers of clothing from his flesh to hers? She told herself sharply to keep her mind on the job, and continued into the room with jaw tight and fists clenched, doing everything she could to fight the stupid crazy languor which had swept over her with so little warning. It wasn't anything he'd done or said, he hadn't given the slightest sign of being aware of her physically. He believed her to be married, and that, as far as he was concerned, was that.

'Get Beth to bring us some tea,' he called back over his shoulder, and closed the door after them.

CHAPTER THREE

SHE wasn't going to think about being here alone with Hobart Rule. Instead she looked round his office, and gradually forgot her confusion in the intriguing contradictions of this sanctuary at the heart of Rule Electronics.

The room itself was predictably lavish, shut off from the city rooftops by tinted glass and filtered air. But, instead of the great desk she would have expected, an old-fashioned oak roll-top stood before the window, lovingly polished but as out of place here as—as a baby's cradle would have been.

She pushed down the thought. The old desk had a modern swivel chair, and was surrounded by shelves of hardware. She noted a personal computer with its keyboard and monitor, and telephones of three colours, but the rest was a bewildering array of switches and dials. She supposed it was mostly office equipment, but he must also play music from that stand of cassettes. It had to be music, he'd hardly want these four loudspeakers about the walls for anything else.

Between herself and the roll-top was a small modern desk, presumably his secretary's, with a swivel chair on either side. She was making for one of these when he redirected her.

'Over here.' He led her to the other end of the room, and pulled back from a walnut table a cane-

seated mahogany chair like those her sea-captain
grandfather had brought from Malaya.

'These all belonged to my parents.' He settled
opposite her in a similar one, and added as he saw
her glancing back. 'Yes, and the desk.'

'They...make an interesting mixture,' she
floundered.

'But they should be in somebody's home,' he
finished the thought for her. 'And that's where
they'll be, when I have one.'

What was he talking about, this millionaire who
had a house and a flat to dispose of? Her bewilderment must have shown.

'You can't buy a home,' he told her, 'through a
house agent.'

Stung by the contempt in his tone, Gemma
flushed. 'Estate agents aren't criminals, Mr Rule.'

'That wasn't the word I had in mind. You must
have known I was selling almost before I knew
myself.'

'I merely rang to enquire...'

'All right, spare me the flannel.'

'Flannel!' Clutching her briefcase, she sprang up.
'I thought we could be helpful to you, Mr Rule,
but I was wrong. You'd better find a firm who
won't mind your rudeness.'

'Sit down!'

She started for the door. 'Where did you learn
to talk like that?' she shot back over her shoulder.
'Dog-obedience classes?'

A quick movement, a rush of air, and he was
blocking her way. She halted because she had to,
or walk into six-feet-plus of solid masculinity.

Angrier with him than ever, she stepped back. To
make matters worse he was smiling, as if amused
at her indignation, but before she could order him
out of her way, the door opened to admit an elegant blonde with a silver tray.

'I'm sorry,' he said to Gemma as if he really
meant it, and turned to the newcomer. 'Thanks,
Beth. On the table, please?'

'Certainly, Mr Rule.'

Beth glided past them with her tray, darting
Gemma a sympathetic sideways glance. She
probably knew this kind of situation all too well;
the man must be a pig to work for.

Or was he? 'How did Clare's birthday party go?'
he was asking now as if he really wanted to know.

'It went a treat, Mr Rule,' Beth replied with good-
natured briskness. 'She loves the teddy you gave
her.'

'And I enjoyed her thank-you letter. I see she's
into purple finger-paint.'

Beth flashed him a smile on her way out. 'Can't
start too soon with the aesthetic bit, can we?'

Gemma listened with mixed feelings. Here it was
again, another easy exchange between Bart Rule
and one of his employees. Perhaps it was this real,
friendly interest of his that kept them working for
him, in spite of his uncertain temper.

'Am I still in trouble?' he asked when they were
alone again.

'I don't know what you mean by trouble,' she
replied coldly.

'I'll keep apologising if you like. I'd no business
to be talking to you like that.' He indicated the tray.

'Have some tea as a peace offering. I'd like to try and explain.'

'There's no need...'

'I need it.' The grey eyes sought hers in complete honesty. 'I'd like to work out for myself why I carried on like that. You come into it somewhere, I think.'

'Do I?'

She tried not to show how intrigued she was, but he must have seen it. He strolled back to the table.

'D'you take milk or sugar?'

'N-neither.' She saw him eye her slenderness, and added sharply, 'I just happen to like it straight.'

'All right, all right.' He poured from a curved silver pot, gestured her back to her seat, and set the tea before her.

She sat very straight, with her briefcase within reach. Only when she was lifting the blue-sprigged cup and saucer did she realise she was doing just what he'd told her, in the place he had chosen for her. She covered her annoyance by sipping the old-fashioned, red-brown brew, and found its freshness soothing.

'I like this porcelain,' she said, glad to find some small talk. 'A good quality china like this doesn't hold the stains.'

'That's exactly what my mother said when she bought it.' His voice was warmer and more relaxed than she had heard it yet today.

'So this belonged to your parents, too?'

'Another refugee looking for a home,' he told her sombrely. 'It's not diswasher-proof, and it wouldn't have gone with the...' He broke off, sighing. 'Mrs Roseveare, I really have nothing against house agents. I just didn't like you being one.'

She put her empty cup on the tray with meticulous care. This was it, the explanation he said she came into somewhere.

'Remember last Saturday?' he went on.

She nodded, scarcely daring to breathe. Had that small incident lingered in his memory as it had in hers?

'With you and your children,' he went on, 'I felt more human than I've done in years.'

'I'm glad you liked us. But . . .'

'I liked you. I kept out to sea after that, just to be away from people, and I guess I sailed too long.' He closed his eyes and shook his head as if to throw off his fatigue. 'But the idea of you all, the idea that families can be happy together, that stayed with me.'

'Mr Rule . . .'

'Then I stagger in here dead-beat, and find you,' his mouth hardened, 'a career lady.'

'Which I have every right to be,' she retorted.

'You have, Mrs Roseveare, but just then I wasn't up to seeing it that way, so I went for you. Sorry again.'

She couldn't doubt his sincerity. 'Th-that's all right,' she murmured, and rushed on to deal with the misunderstanding which really must be cleared up, 'but those were my sister's children.'

He blinked, and regarded her with eyes suddenly hooded. 'And you've none of your own, Mrs Roseveare?'

'I'm not married, Mr Rule.'

The statement hung in the air between them, and she waited to see how it would affect him. His re-action when it came was not the one she was used to.

'Your sister's children?' He smiled at the memory. 'You were great with them.'

'So were you,' she assured him, glad to be able to return the compliment. 'They talked about you for hours.'

'Did they?' He seemed absurdly pleased. 'I thought about them, too. About all three of you, so close, so happy...' He broke off and turned to stare out of the window.

Gemma never knew what came over her then. Something about the high-nosed Cornish profile, lost in thoughts that were miles from this city office, made her forget herself completely.

Before she knew what she was doing she had leant across the polished table and offered him both her hands. Equally unthinking, he took them in a strong, gentle grip that felt safe and right as home. The dry conditioned air seemed to blow softer round them, like the wind of a Cornish beach.

Then his hands closed tighter and it happened again, that sharp current from flesh to flesh. She felt the hair at the nape of her neck prickle, the blood hammer in her ears and rush to the surface of her skin, until even her throat and shoulders were burning; she hadn't blushed like this since she was a schoolgirl. She snatched her hands back and looked for something, anything, to occupy them.

Thank goodness for her briefcase. She opened it and riffled through it, making an unnecessary fuss of the job of locating her notebook and pen, though they were exactly where she always kept them. When she had put her cup and saucer on the tray, set the notebook on the table in front of her, and placed the pen very carefully beside it, she was almost ready to face him again.

And knew at once that her frantic activity hadn't begun to take him in. She'd given herself away and he knew it. Yes, he knew it all now, not only that she wasn't married, but that she wasn't really here on business. She looked down at her notebook, refusing to meet the new challenge in those clear-sighted eyes.

'You're called Gemma, aren't you?'

She generally let clients make their own decisions about first names. Not trusting her voice, she nodded.

'I'm glad you're here, Gemma.'

'Are you?' It came out with a husky tremor.

'And not only because you're so beautiful.'

'B-beautiful?'

She had to look up. Those disquieting eyes were fixed on hers and she knew it wasn't just an idle compliment, the battered coinage of a man on the make. No, he was telling the simple truth that he was glad to see her again and that her looks pleased him, no more and no less.

'Sh-shall we...' She cleared her throat and tried again. 'Shall we start with your flat, Mr Rule?'

'No, we'll start by you calling me Bart.'

'I am sort of used to it,' she admitted. 'In our part of Cornwall everybody calls you that.'

'I know. And what do they call you, Miss Roseveare?'

She hesitated, flustered. 'I don't use my Cornish name.'

What on earth had made her say that? Normally she didn't even give away that she had one. Furious with herself, she met his interested gaze and prepared to fight off all questions.

'Well?' he prompted. 'Aren't you going to tell me it?'

'Certainly not. I don't like it.'

He smiled, mocking her defensiveness, serenely convinced he'd make his own decisions about what to call her. 'We don't always get what we like.'

'What, not even if you're a . . .'

She stopped, appalled at herself. Whatever had come over her, letting him provoke her like this? One of the first things she'd ever had to learn was that the customer was always right. And she'd had enough experience of the rich to know how often they hated to be reminded how rich they were.

The mocking smile continued. 'You were about to say, if you're a millionaire?'

She compressed her lips. She mustn't let him needle her into any more gaffes like that.

'Don't worry, you're not the first to remind me. Not by a long way.' He added with a chuckle, 'Maybe I need it.'

'The flat.' She unclipped the pen she had put alongside her notebook. 'It's in Belgravia, you said?'

'No, you don't, Gemma Roseveare.'

She sighed and tapped the pen on the notebook, signalling how patient she was being. 'Don't what?'

'Don't pretend it's all in a day's work,' he threw the words down like a challenge, 'when we both know you came here because you wanted to see me again.'

'Wha-at?' Startled out of her cool pose, she choked on the word, eyes wide in dismay. 'Mr Rule...'

'Bart.'

'Mr Rule, have you any idea of professional etiquette?'

'I have, Miss Roseveare, I have. And if that had been my only idea,' he jerked his head in the direction of the outer office, 'you'd never have got through the door.'

She found the pen clammy in her grip, and put it carefully on the table in front of her. 'Would you mind explaining that?'

'Certainly. You've heard of Rule Holdings?'

She nodded. 'Mr Derby mentioned them.'

'I thought he might. So let's just say that the director of Rule Holdings doesn't need house agents.'

'I see.' She picked up her pen and notebook, dropped them back in her briefcase, and brought it up to her lap.

'I'm sorry to have wasted your time then, Mr Rule,' she bit off in the words in clipped precision. 'It was nice meeting you.'

She watched stonily as he laughed aloud.

'I'm glad you're not disappointed, Miss Roseveare.'

'I wouldn't say that.' She closed the hard, leather-covered lid on all her hopes of doing a deal with this infuriating man. 'If I didn't have to get back to my office, I might tell you a thing or two.'

'Tell away.'

'Oh, I'm much too busy for that.' She settled her jacket over her hips, ready to stand up.

'This is where I'm supposed to apologise again, isn't it?' he asked imperturbably. 'Well, I'm not going to.'

'That's up to you. Goodnight, Mr Rule.'

She rose to her feet, and discovered too late that she hadn't fastened her briefcase. Her quick movement was all it needed for the lid to fall open and fill with a cascade of rubber bands and string and twopence coins and paperclips, the button she'd been meaning to sew back on her coat and the ring with the loose stone, the safety-pin for emergencies and the half-filled income-tax form which should have been posted six weeks ago, all higgledy-piggledy over the neatly stowed tools of her trade.

She made a grab to close it, but only managed to dislodge the shiny green apple she always kept for when she grew hungrier than she could bear. Fuming as she wrestled with the unbalanced briefcase, she watched the apple roll over her papers, teeter on the hard edge of the lid, and thump quietly to the heavy-pile carpet.

Before she could pick it up he was at her side, down on one knee as if for an old-fashioned proposal of marriage, and holding the apple up to her like a bouquet. 'Yours, I believe?'

They were the same words he'd used when they first met. Yes, and he knew it, she was sure of that as she dumped the briefcase on her chair and grabbed the apple from him.

Remembering her determination to be polite at all costs, she managed a muttered, 'Th-thank you.'

'Don't mention it.' He watched her efforts with cool enjoyment. 'It's standing on your dignity that does it.'

'I wasn't...'

'I notice it myself, whenever I get on my high horse.'

'I wasn't...' She bit her lip, realising the uselessness of arguing with him. 'Mr Rule!'

'Bart.'

'Mr Rule,' she threw the loose clutter back from the lid into the box of the briefcase and banged it shut, looking down on him with something like desperation, 'will you please get up, and move out of my way?'

'Well, perhaps I'll get up, anyway.'

He rose smoothly to his feet and everything was suddenly worse. She had forgotten how he towered over her own five foot three, how hard and yet supple he was with that length of limb and breadth of shoulder. The blue-grey jacket only hinted at the taut waist beneath, but the soft blue cotton of his jeans gave full play to the narrow lines of his hips. She looked away hastily.

And uselessly. While she bent over the briefcase, busying herself with the job of making sure the locks really were closed this time, she felt a firm hand on each elbow.

'Stop that. We need to talk.'

Then he was drawing her upright, and hemming her in worse than ever. She was far too close to him, close enough to see the tiny scar on his cheek and the individual strands that made up the wiry lock of hair over his forehead. She watched the white teeth part for a healthy pink tongue to dart over the long, humorous lips, and then she couldn't look at his mouth any more. But that only brought her to his eyes, clear grey eyes that seemed ready to draw her in and drown her, eyes that blazed into hers and brought an answering heat... No, she couldn't look into his eyes.

But she couldn't turn away from them, either. She couldn't turn away from him, though his hold on her had relaxed to the mere cradling of her elbows in his palms. His touch was striking sparks into her blood, yet she could easily have shaken his hands off if she had only felt strong enough. She didn't feel strong enough. The gentle pressure of his thumbs, distant as a handshake, tantalising as a caress, warmed the silk of her dress over the sensitive skin of her inner arms, and drained her will.

'Listen, Gemma Roseveare,' his voice was slow but decisive, 'you've put me through hoops, this past half-hour.'

She stiffened and drew herself up, but that brought her eyes to the long, determined mouth. She turned her head away.

'Will you...' It came out a croak, so she started again. 'Will you please let go of me?'

'Certainly.'

He dropped his hands, and she had to wrestle with a strange new feeling deep within her. Now he was no longer touching her the world seemed colder, less welcoming than it ever had before. I wanted him to kiss me, she thought in panic. It's what I've wanted ever since I first set eyes on him.

'I've wanted to kiss you ever since I first set eyes on you,' he echoed as if he'd got right inside her head. 'Only, I happen to think marriage is important.'

'It wasn't my fault you thought I was married.'

'But I did, and it distracted me, for a while. That's why it's taken me so long to work you out.'

'There's nothing to work out.'

'Oh, yes, there is, Gemma Roseveare. More than you know,' he continued remorselessly. 'You're a very mixed-up lady.'

'I am not! And if you think marriage is so important,' she added, glad to find something she could throw back at him, 'why did you see me at all? If you didn't want an estate agent, and you *did* want to...to...'

'To kiss you,' he finished her sentence coolly. 'Don't worry, I'm in full control of that side of things.'

'I'm glad to hear it,' she snapped, tight-lipped with a disappointment she wouldn't admit.

'No, you're not, but we'll leave that for now. I asked you in here because,' he shrugged, 'I was tired, miserable, at a loose end. I thought I might enjoy just talking to you.'

'Honoured, I'm sure.'

'Don't spar. It doesn't get us anywhere.'

'And where precisely do you think we're going?'

'An interesting question.' He glanced down at the chair she had vacated, her newly locked briefcase lying on it as if butter wouldn't melt in its mouth. 'I don't suppose you'd sit down again and let us talk this through sensibly?'

'You forget, I'm on my way out.'

'You aren't, you know.'

'I wish you'd stop contradicting me, Mr Rule!'

'Bart. And I'm sorry to go on contradicting you, but you're staying.' He gave her a sudden grin, white teeth flashing in the dark-tanned face. 'Until we've got to know each other better. That's the whole idea.'

'Whose idea?' she demanded, and regretted it at once. Sure enough, he jumped straight into the opening she'd given him.

'Yours, to start with. But I've caught up with you.'

Then his hands were gentle on her waist. She could easily have pulled away, only those eyes, that mouth...

The kiss was like coming home after a weary journey. His lips held hers while his arms walled her in, and for a long moment that was enough. Then she parted her lips, tasted the salt of his, met his answering tongue while she drew closer to him and fitted her body to his, felt the strength of him offered to her like another part of her being never understood till now. How could she not have understood it till now, this closeness, when she had been seeking it all her life?

It was Bart who put her away from him, his gentle murmur which brought her back to the real world. 'Yes, Gemma Roseveare, I've caught up with you.'

She would have liked to exclaim at his arrogance, to order him brusquely to take his hands off her, but she didn't have the chance. Before she could collect her shattered composure he was at the table, gathering things on the tea-tray.

'You were out of my reach. A beautiful memory.' He put his cup in hers, and laid both sideways on the same saucer. 'I'm glad you found a reason for seeing me, and sorted me out on that.'

'I came to discuss property, Mr Rule.'

'And if that hadn't worked, you'd have found something else.'

'And what a fool I'd have been,' she burst out, affronted at his downright way of putting it.

'But it did work. We've met.' He turned on her the full force of those sea-grey eyes. 'And I'm not letting you go yet awhile, Gemma Roseveare.'

'Do I get a say in it, Mr Rule?'

At last he showed irritation. 'For goodness' sake, Gemma, what does it take to make you use my first name?'

'A little politeness would help.'

'A little less honesty, you mean.' He glanced at his watch. 'Look, I've got to talk to Jim before he goes.'

'Don't let me keep you.'

'I may not have a choice.' He surveyed her for a moment, and went on with a sigh, 'You've got me, that's for sure. Whether you keep me is something we'll have to find out.'

'You're talking riddles, Bart Rule.'

'And you know what I'm talking about, Gemma Roseveare.'

She raised her chin, meaning to return him stare for stare. But once she was really looking at him again her resentment flickered and died, unable to survive its contact with that open grey gaze. For a moment their eyes communicated without words, and expressed what couldn't have been put into words. She saw the complexity of his feelings about her, that he was sexually drawn to her in spite of himself, against his better judgement almost.

He's been hurt, she thought. I wonder who hurt him? And had to fight the urge to put her arms round him and comfort him, assure him that, whatever any woman had done to him in the past, with her it would be different.

But he wasn't asking for any reassurance, and didn't need it. He was a man who enjoyed taking risks, who would launch himself on the ski-run for the sheer exhilaration of it.

She had to smile at the absurd turn her thoughts had taken.

'That's better.' He let the words fall into the lengthening silence. 'You should smile more often, Gemma Roseveare.'

'I smile when I have something to smile at, Bart Rule. I was thinking of us as starting down a ski-run.'

'That's not so far out.' He chuckled, considering the idea. 'Cold, dangerous...'

'Thank you!'

'But exciting. And once you're on it, no going back.' His laughter ceased, and he held her gaze. 'There's more to us than that though, lots more. And I'm going to discover it.'

'Are you, Bart?'

'Let me spell it out,' he began, his eyes kindling at her use of his name. 'We like each other. No,' he turned away and pulled at his hair as if forcing himself to concentrate, 'I'll have to think of another way of putting it. Seeing that's exactly what we're not sure about.'

'What is?' she asked, not believing she'd heard right.

'If there's any real liking in it,' he explained matter-of-factly. 'All we know so far is how very much we fancy each other.'

'Are you having the nerve to say you don't like me?'

'Silly!' He smiled at her indignation. 'I'm talking about honouring, respecting, thinking well of. I don't know about any of those yet. Do you?'

There he went again, putting things into words that should not be spoken. 'Thank you, Bart Rule,' she said at last. 'You certainly know how to make a woman feel courted.'

'That's a nice old-fashioned word.' His voice was full of a pleasure quite without irony.

'My mother's,' she realised with surprise. 'I've never wanted to use it before.'

'Maybe you've never been courted before.'

'And I am now?'

'Let's try it. What are you doing this evening?'

She stared out of the tinted window, thinking of her empty flat. She ought to finish her unpacking. And she was hoping for a call from the buyer interested in the Kensington place. And she had to ring the seller who had been out all day and hadn't left a key.

'Come on, Gemma, give a guy a break,' he urged her softly. 'My holiday was in ruins, till you turned up.'

She recalled his abrupt arrival in Mr Derby's office. 'Are you still supposed to be on it?'

'Somewhere in the English Channel,' he confirmed.

'It's a lot to expect of a woman, to stand in for the English Channel.'

'You can do it, Gemma Roseveare. Have dinner with me?'

Raising her eyes and giving him look for look, she resisted no longer. 'Thanks, Bart. I'd like that.'

CHAPTER FOUR

GEMMA was surprised at the place Bart chose to take her. When she told him she had letters to sign, and wouldn't be able to go home and change, his glance lingered on the leaf-patterned silk of her dress.

'You look gorgeous, anyway. Do you mind walking?'

'Love it,' she told him truthfully.

'Seven o'clock then, at your office?'

'Right. It's one of those Victorian houses, round the corner from the park...'

'I can read a street-plan,' he cut her short.

And sure enough, at exactly seven o'clock, still in his shore-going yachtsman's gear, he ascended the steps to the great front door of Drew Brothers. Together they walked a brisk half-mile of summer streets, chatting of St Austell and Fowey and sailing, to a comfortable pub where the middle-aged man behind the bar greeting them in unmistakably Cornish accents.

'Gemma,' Bart said, 'this is Chief Petty Officer Hawkins, RN, retired. When will it be ready, Chief?'

'Give it half an hour,' the man replied. 'Just nice time for you to settle down.'

'It's roast beef,' Bart told Gemma, and turned back to the Chief. 'With all the trimmings?'

'All there.' Chief drew a pint for a newly arrived customer. 'We got the vegetables in from the garden after you phoned.'

More customers appeared, and Bart indicated a side door. 'We'll go and make ourselves comfortable, then, shall we?'

The restaurant was empty, but by the sunny garden window a table had been set for two. Gemma inhaled the perfume of deep yellow rosebuds in a delicate vase, and of wax from candles of exactly the same deep yellow, in holders of the same porcelain.

'Stylish!'

'That's in your honour.' He drew out a chair for her from the heavy damask cloth laid with silver tableware.

'Oh, yes?' She eyed him disbelievingly. 'It's nothing to do with Rule Electronics, then?'

'I don't do business entertaining here, if that's what you mean.' He settled opposite. 'Generally, I eat with the family.'

'Family? In a pub?'

'Oh, well, they're grown up now. But Chief always made time for his family. I suppose,' his eyes were suddenly veiled, 'it's one of the things I like about him.'

'You've known him a long time, then?'

'Getting on.' He looked approvingly at the bottle of Côtes-du-Rhône in its silver stand, cork already drawn. 'Would you like an aperitif? Or shall we start this straight away?'

'Straight away, please.'

She watched with enjoyment as he tried the dark red wine, then poured it deftly into the long-stemmed glasses. Hunger always sharpened her senses at this time of day, and she revelled in the knowledge that she hadn't yet drunk either of the two glasses of wine she allowed herself per week. Maybe she would binge them both here and now.

The smell of French dressing from the classically served avocado on her plate was more than she could bear. 'Er...shall we begin?'

'Let's.' He put down the glass he had been cradling between his hands. 'I like a woman who can eat.'

She took it in, but refused to let it come between her and the luscious perfection of the avocado. She would do just as she always did, eat what fitted in with her diet chart. And if that disappointed him, too bad.

Their first course finished, he plugged in the heated tray and stood up. 'Will you excuse me a moment?' He neatly removed the used plates. 'They're much too busy in the bar at this time of the evening to wait on us.'

'But what about the restaurant staff?'

'The restaurant's closed today—hadn't you gathered?' He nodded round at the empty tables. 'I told you, this is family supper we're having.'

He left her wondering. What was it about this millionaire, this man of power, who could eat in any exotic restaurant he chose, that made him choose to bring her to an obscure pub and give her a meal he had to serve himself? Then the scent of roast beef wafted to her, and she decided this way of doing things made sense, after all. What could be better than really good home cooking?

The silver platter he was bearing from the kitchen held flawlessly carved slices of sirloin, baby carrots, young runner beans, and roast potatoes whose golden shine almost broke her will. She watched hungrily as he set down a sauce-boat of horse-radish, and forced herself to look away from the plate of small, individual Yorkshire puddings which presently joined it.

'Madam.'

He set a warmed porcelain plate in front of her, and flourished the serving spoons. She took them with enthusiasm, put meat, carrots, and runner beans on her plate, and before he had sat down was waiting impatiently for him to serve himself.

'Is that all you're having?' he asked in surprise.

'It's enough. Do take what you want, so we can start.'

He shrugged, and began to organise food on to his plate.

Normally Gemma managed to eat slowly, savouring every small mouthful in the manner laid down by her diet books. But this beef was so tender and so full of juice, these vegetables so superbly themselves that, try as she would, she couldn't help finishing them far more quickly than she ought. She put her knife and fork down before Bart was even half-way through his plateful.

'Have some more?' He poured her second glass of wine.

'Well . . .' Bother it, she'd just have to cut down later in the week. She didn't often get the chance of food like this.

Her second helping was half finished before she remembered she was already supposed to be fasting, to make up for the weekend with the family. To make matters worse, he was eyeing her with clear disapproval.

'I shouldn't have thought you'd need to diet.'

'Everybody needs to diet,' she told him crisply.

'I don't.'

Watching him give his attention again to his food, she had to admit he might be right. He was lean and spare as a hunting animal; you'd think he'd always had to fight for every mouthful. Perhaps in a sense he had—but just the same, he must be one of those lucky people who burned off all their calories. She sighed, her plate empty for a second time, and allowed herself a glance—just one glance each—at the potatoes and the Yorkshire puddings.

'And neither do you.' His first helping finished, he took the subject up where they had left it. 'You're far too skinny.'

'Skinny?' she repeated in outrage. 'I am not!'

'Well, maybe not. In fact, you're a very nice shape.' He eyed what he could see of it above the table as he prepared to replenish his plate. 'You just need filling out a bit.'

'Kindly keep your personal remarks to yourself,' she told him stiffly. 'How would you like it if I talked about those awful old clothes you were wearing on Saturday?'

'I shouldn't mind. I was wearing those to be comfortable. He paused, serving spoon in hand. 'It's not like starving yourself for no reason at all.'

She couldn't help being reminded of her reflection as she had studied it early this afternoon. The word 'starved' had come into her mind then, and now this infuriating man was using it aloud. Goaded, she snapped at him.

'My reasons are my own affair.'

'They're clear for all the world to see,' he answered tranquilly. 'You want to be skinny.'

'You said I wasn't...'

'You aren't—yet.'

The sinister emphasis he put on the last word was so disturbing that she had to ask, 'What do you mean, "yet"?'

'It's only a matter of time.'

About to retort, she stopped to swallow. She had just caught a whiff of the roast potato he had lifted on the serving spoon, and didn't know how to bear it. And the pile of Yorkshire pudding had scarcely been dented.

She looked determinedly away from them, but that only brought her back to his mocking eyes. She could feel his glance taking in the hollows under her cheekbones, the sharper hollows revealed at the base of her throat by the V-neck of her dress, the small bones of her wrist tense under their thin covering of flesh.

She swallowed again, and practically snarled, 'You are the rudest man...'

'I see now why you're so bad-tempered. You don't eat enough.'

'Mr Rule...'

'Here we go again.' He put down the serving spoons. 'Shall I tell you what you remind me of?'

'I don't want to know...'

'That marvellous film—what's it called?—*The African Queen*.' He sat back, surveying her again. 'Ten years from now, you're going to be exactly what Humphrey Bogart called Katherine Hepburn—a skinny old maid.'

That did it. To deal with a man like this, you needed your strength. She snatched the serving spoons, put two potatoes on her plate, and quickly added two Yorkshire puddings. And it would have been a crime to eat them without the things that were meant to be eaten with them, so she took a third slice of meat, and this time garnished it with a liberal dollop of horseradish.

Her deprived palate detected the cream in the horseradish at once, and revelled in it. And the Yorkshire puddings lived up to every word of the popular Yorkshire poem: as light as the down on the breast of a dove. As for those potatoes... She stopped thinking, and gave herself up to pure enjoyment.

Where had everything gone? She asked herself the question as she finished the last lick of her last helping of sherry trifle, but her satisfied stomach was already telling her the answer. They hadn't talked much, just helped each other to one more spoonful of this or that, and as the food had disappeared so the mood between them had relaxed. She could see it in the comfortable way he was sitting, one arm on the table, playing with the stem of his empty wineglass while his eyes gazed lazily into hers.

When he offered her brandy or a liqueur, she shook her head.

'I really do draw the line at spirits.'

'Coffee, then?'

Again she shook her head. 'What I really want...' She broke off, aware of his eyes on her mouth, aware of her own tongue moistening her lips, and of his eyes following the small movement.

'Is a fast walk,' she finished briskly, 'to...' Help me be sensible, she'd meant say, but caught it back in time. 'To give my digestion a chance.'

He grinned. 'Where shall it be, then?'

She saw at once that he understood. Understood how she had been entangled for a moment, just as he had, in the other side of their developing relationship, the physical side. And understood too that she didn't want to put any of those thoughts into words. When she next spoke, it was out of a great rush of gratitude for his quick comprehension.

'I live in St John's Wood.'

She paused, worried again at what she was getting into. But this evening, this whole day had been one of burning bridges, giving in to her instincts, launching herself on the downward slope and seeing where it would carry her. She might as well finish what she had begun.

'The distance is just right for walking,' she went on, looking him full in the eyes. 'We could have coffee at my flat.'

He kept his gaze on hers. 'I'd like that.'

In the streets, blue-green lamps were just winking into life against the fading sunset and the lights coming on in the houses. Rooms with curtains not yet drawn showed bright table-lamps, flowers, walls hung with pictures.

'Cosy!' Bart's voice had a world of yearning, as if he had spent a lifetime like this, looking in from the outside.

Before she knew it Gemma had drawn closer to him in the soft darkness and slipped her hand into his. 'These houses are very small, you know. It makes them inconvenient in lots of ways.'

His hand closed warm round hers, but his voice came now with a certain dryness. 'You mean, they may look nice, but I wouldn't be so thrilled if I had to live there?'

'Something like that,' she admitted.

'Don't bank on it. Big places have their draw-backs, too. Our...' he stopped, and corrected himself. '*My* town flat has eight bedrooms, five bathrooms, two kitchens...'

'You certainly aren't pushed for space.' She spoke more to show she was still with him than from any real interest in the splendours of his flat. He wasn't boasting, rather the opposite, and in the course of her work she dealt with many equally big homes.

'When we bought it,' he went on, 'it was adver-tised as "ideal for family occupation".'

She flinched at the sarcastic parody of what he would have called house agents' jargon. But his hand had tightened round hers, helping her to say quietly, 'I gather it wasn't?'

'What it turned out to be ideal for was Adam fireplaces, Venetian chandeliers, Sheraton cabinets . . .'

'I know the kind of thing.'

'Professionally, you mean? That's about the only way there is to know them.' He had quickened his pace, pulling her along beside him on the dim-lit pavement. 'They're professionally decorated, and then they're used for professional entertaining, by professional . . . personalities.'

They walked the length of another street in silence. Gemma was wondering for the first time about Caroline Lang, who had been his wife. The whole nation had recognized and applauded her gift for shrewd questions in the television interviews she conducted so coolly. Had that same shrewdness led her to choose their flat, have it decorated as the perfect setting for her pale beauty, and entertain in it to further her career? But why not? As a career-woman herself, Gemma had to sympathise.

Yet still she wanted to comfort Bart. She remembered the old roll-top desk in his office, and the other furniture which should have been in his home. Why on earth hadn't he insisted on it?

But, even as she asked herself the question, she knew the answer. They looked strange in his office, but at least they were under his loving eye; he had daily contact with them. They could never have fitted into the glossy showplace he had just described. And those old bits and pieces were part of his life. He loved them. How could he make an argument over them and force them into alien surroundings which would only have emphasised their shabbiness? It would have been like . . . like leaving your baby in an institution.

Babies again! Almost, she was glad to reach the big front door of Linden House. With a mixture of apprehension and relief, she released her hand from Bart's to find her keys. As she opened the street door, she began to speak too quickly.

'I'm afraid my place isn't as tidy as it might be...'

'Calm down.' He closed the door behind them. 'You know things like that needn't worry you.'

'Oh, needn't they?' she snapped, reacting sharply as ever against his commanding tone and his habit of stating everything in so many words. 'And what, in your opinion,' she led the way into the lift and pushed the button, 'should I be worrying about?'

'Us,' he answered simply as the lift started on its way, 'and what we're going to do about each other.'

Silenced again, she waited for the second-floor doors to open and release her from this narrow space where they had to stand so close. In her own hallway she switched on the light and turned towards her tiny kitchen.

'That's the living-room.' She indicated with a nod. 'I'll be there in a minute.'

When he was safely into it and away from her, she slid out of her jacket and hung it on one of the hall pegs. She had offered him coffee and she was going to make it, whatever he thought he'd come for. The small task of pouring water into the machine was already working its soothing magic, and the good smell of the coffee as she measured it into the filter made her feel almost normal. After all, there were other things in life besides this maddening masculine presence in her living-room.

Only when she joined him there did she lose courage again. She had forgotten how big he was, and it had never occurred to her how he would dwarf her lovingly arranged furniture. She could see why he'd chosen the couch, it was the only place on which he had the least hope of being comfortable, and even then he had to stay sideways on it so as not to collide with her Benares brass coffee-table. Yes, and if he ventured too near the other end of it his shoulder would knock into the wall-lamp she used for reading. It was like—like being in a parlour with a stallion.

She turned away hurriedly, shutting off that line of thought before it could lead her into more trouble. But the turning away brought her face-to-face with her calendar of famous paintings, and this month's picture would just have to be 'Joy', wouldn't it? She jerked away from Klimt's naked lovers in their rainbow dreamworld, and took the old-fashioned granny chair which usually fitted its corner so well and now seemed absurdly small.

'Right then.' He resumed the conversation as if they had never dropped it. 'What are we going to do about us?'

She shrugged. 'The coffee'll be ready in a minute.'

'Stop dodging!'

'Coffee,' she sat very upright, 'is what I invited you for.'

'No, it isn't. However,' he stretched hugely, legs just clear of the brass tray and lengthening endlessly across the carpet, arms making a great muscular sweep above his head. 'if you want to leave that can of worms for tonight...'

'*Can of worms?* You have such a turn of phrase!'

'Sorry.' He grinned at her outrage. 'You know what I mean.'

'No, I don't. Tell me.'

He sighed, and explained as if for the fifteenth time to a slow learner. 'You and I, my darling, are violently attracted to each other.'

'Speak for yourself.'

'For goodness' sake, Gemma! How can we get anywhere if you won't admit that, at least?'

'I—I'm not in the habit of...' She choked to a halt.

'You don't sleep around? Of course not,' he surveyed her coolly. 'Neither do I. And I'm certainly not here to wheedle my way into your bed.'

'Oh, you...'

Once more, she couldn't go on. Did he expect her to say everything outright as he did? Tell him she wanted to make love, that the very sight of him, the great male turbulence in this room which until now had been entirely hers, was battering down any resistance she might have had?

'What is all this?' The level grey gaze was seeking hers again. 'What's got you on your high horse this time?'

'I... I'll go and see if the coffee's ready.'

Standing up and whirling angrily towards the door, she must have caught the tall, stiff calendar and dislodged it from its nail. She found it balancing upright on her shoulder like a fantastic parrot, until it reversed itself in a flutter of pages and slid down the front of her dress. She made a grab and nearly fell with it.

'Careful!' His supporting hand burnt through the silk at her waist. 'You'll have that brass tray-thing over next.'

His other hand was at her back, and she felt herself gently lowered to his side while the calendar thumped to the floor. She leant to pick it up and then, still poised forward with arm out, knew she had no more choice.

Perhaps she'd never had one. Perhaps it had always been like this, his stillness and warmth and strength and excitement reaching out to her as surely as if he had pulled her into his arms. When she turned back to him, there was only one thing to do.

This time his kisses were hard and hungry, as if his lips could never have enough of hers, letting them go only to taste instead her cheeks, her ears, her eyes, her neck. She sighed and shuddered, sending her hands to savour the breadth of his chest, the strong framework of each shoulder-blade through the fabric of the striped shirt.

His fingers tangled in her hair, followed the contours of her head to the nape of her neck, lingered there, drew slowly round and possessed themselves of her breast. Cradling its weight, he played with the urgent nipple through the silk until she moaned and reached for her side zip, thinking of nothing but the need to open herself to his caresses.

Her hand closed instead on that wretched piece of paper, the drawing which had shown her more about herself than she wanted to know. Now it was doing worse, reminding her how totally unprepared she was for this encounter.

There had been no need, no men in her life, for so many years. She could feel his touch like tracks of fire in her hair and her neck and now her breast, fire and sweetness flowing through her and almost drowning her senses. Nothing mattered, nothing at all, but to pull him into her and complete the pattern, let them drown together as one. Maybe, she thought incoherently as she sought his mouth again, maybe it would be all right. And if it wasn't, that would be all right, too. She'd have a baby...

It was the actual word in her mind which pulled her up short. She struggled away, fighting herself rather than him.

'What am I doing? Please...'

'I think you know, my darling.' He released her, and added more briskly, though still a little husky-voiced, 'What about that coffee?'

She escaped to the kitchen without a word, and in the small tasks of arranging and pouring regained some of her composure. She couldn't help thinking of Kevin, the only other man with whom she had forgotten herself like this. What was it Bart had said about not wheedling his way into her bed? Kevin had wheedled, and stormed, and sulked. He'd even called her an ugly name, and told her no man would put up with her kind of behaviour. And she'd believed him.

'I'm sorry.' She handed Bart his cup and took hers carefully to the granny chair. 'I didn't mean that to happen.'

'Nothing happened.' He was already himself again, leaning back with easy grace in the narrow space at his disposal. 'And nothing will, until you're ready.'

She wondered if he had any idea how very ready she'd been, ready beyond all caution and good sense. She dared to glance at him, but the storm-grey eyes were peaceful as ever, and she knew he spoke only to soothe and calm her.

'We've just met,' he reminded her gently. 'Neither of us knows yet where we want this to go.'

There he went again, back to the question of whether any real liking existed between them. She opened her mouth for a sharp retort, but quickly closed it. After all, he had just shown restraint and kindness, and she was grateful for it.

'Wh-where had you in mind?' she asked instead.

'Let's cruise along for a bit, and see what happens.' He gave her a lazy grin, then sat up as his choice of words sank in on him. 'That's a thought. How are you on sailing boats?'

'I can cope.' She spoke laconically, and hoped he couldn't hear the thumping of her heart. Was he really going to invite her on board the *Felicity*?

He was. 'How about sailing to Cherbourg with me, then?'

'When?' She tried to control her eagerness. 'This weekend?'

'Sorry, no.' He pulled out a diary and consulted it. 'I have to be there by then.'

'Have to?' she queried sceptically.

'It's business. Though I won't deny I'm expecting to enjoy it, too—especially if you're there.'

To be at sea in this June weather! For a moment her mind filled with longing, with pictures of the two of them, alone, gilded by the sun, idling through blue sea on a white boat. Reluctantly she abandoned them.

'I can't. I'd never get away at such short notice.'

'Perhaps it's just as well.' He gave her a teasing look from under the heavy eyebrows. 'There's nothing like a small boat for showing up the worst in people.'

She bridled. 'Isn't there, indeed? And what worst do you expect to be shown?'

'I don't know. But supposing you decide to call me,' he stuck his nose in the air and put on a mincing falsetto, '*Mr Rule*, all the way.'

'You could certainly make me want to, being so rude.'

'Rude? Me?' He acted comic astonishment. 'Never. Unless maybe you steered us into a collision with a tanker.'

'As if I would,' she began indignantly, and stopped. 'You'd let me steer?'

'Somebody has to.'

'You put it so graciously. All the same.' She sighed at the thought of hot, noisy streets instead of lapping water, and of endless purposeful dialogues with owners and buyers instead of this easy banter. 'I wish I could get the time off.'

'Why don't you try asking for it?'

'I wouldn't need to do that,' she corrected him with dignity. 'I do my own organising.'

'There you are, then.'

'I see what you mean.' And she did at last see that it was up to her whether she went on the *Felicity* or not. 'Where are you moored?'

'A tiny landing-place at the far end of the Solent. I'm driving down tomorrow.'

'How would it be if I joined you there in the evening?'

'Fine. I'd spend the day stocking up, then meet your train.'

She hardly listened, busy with ideas for a quick reshuffle of her commitments. Supposing she sent one of her assistants to the house in Wandsworth and the other to Kevin's flat? She would use her own know-how to put the final word to the write-ups when they were in. The Hampstead deal wouldn't want attention for a week or two, and if she skipped her walk she could settle the Kensington one. As for the partners, the brothers Drew themselves, after her long years of unblemished reliability they would just have to bear it this once if she took some leave at short notice.

'I can do it,' she said triumphantly. 'I'll have the rest of this week, and ring the office on Friday.'

'That's great.'

His chuckle, she suspected, was partly amusement at the way she had suddenly discovered she was her own master. But she couldn't doubt his pleasure at her decision.

'Right,' he went on. 'Here's how we'll do it...'

After she had fetched her railway timetable from her bedroom, and they had decided which train she would catch, it was high time for her to take her keys and see him to the street door. Returning to

her flat with his gentle goodnight kiss burning on
her cheek, she moved dreamily into her bedroom
and put her hand to the zip of her dress.

And there it was again, that wretched piece of
paper with the drawing which showed her deepest,
most secret desire. The thing she wanted most in
the world and until now had never admitted.

She sat on her narrow bed, and smoothed it open
on her lap to confront it squarely at last.

CHAPTER FIVE

'AFTER all,' she said to herself, 'why not? Why shouldn't I have a child of my own?'

All her own, with no husband to get in her way with his demands. Plenty of women did, by accident or design, and neither they nor the children were any the worse for it.

She could do it. Especially if she finally made that long-delayed move back home, and started her own business there as she had meant for years to do some day. If she did that, she could have a house instead of a flat, good air, a garden, her parents to help.

Oh, dear, she thought, brought to a full stop for a moment. My parents!

Still, they had to come into the twentieth century some time. They would see how well she managed, and even they would have to admit that a woman didn't need the complications of marriage before she allowed herself the fulfilment of motherhood.

But would she really be able to manage so well? It would mean a lot of hard work. Professionally, she'd be on her own, responsible for everything in a small office and doing her best to get a new business off the ground. And at home, she'd have a bigger place and a child to care for. She might be able to hire some domestic help, but she wasn't sure. Money would be tight and she might need all she could spare to pay a child-minder and later nursery school.

She opened the window to clear her head, but the waxing moon and the flawless stars merely confused her. Instead of planning ways and means, she found she was staring up at the velvet sky and dreaming, dreaming of what a marvellous way it would be to conceive a child, out on the water with Bart Rule.

Bart!

She came inside again and closed the window firmly, eyes wide. He had to be the father, she couldn't bear the idea of anyone else, and if it was a boy she wanted it to be just like him. But shouldn't she tell him? Hadn't he the right to share this decision with her?

Certainly not, she decided firmly. That's the whole point, to keep my life clear of men. It's my body, my decision, my baby. I'll do as I please.

Besides, another worry was nagging at her. If she told him what she had in mind, he might find it quite hard to believe she wanted just that and nothing else. A new, sordid thought had come to her, and had to be faced. He might think it was all a device to make money from him.

His riches and power were such a magnet. So many people must have been drawn by them, blind to anything else he was or did. He must have experienced so many kinds of falseness in business, in friendship, in sexual dealings—perhaps even in marriage. With his shrewd judgement he was bound to be cynical by now, on the look-out all the time, perhaps even unconsciously, for new attempts to manipulate him.

He might even—hanging up her dress, she paused in horror—he might even think I'm looking to marry him because he's rich.

All right, she herself knew the idea was absurd, but she couldn't expect him to realise it. He didn't know how settled she was, how determined never to waste her time with anything so messy and uncomfortable as another live-in male. So determined that she had actually gone to the trouble of seeking him out, simply to prove to herself that he was only a man like the rest, with all a man's tiresome ways.

She knew why she'd done that, but he didn't. As he saw it, only her initiative had brought them together again, when he had believed her cut off from him by a happy marriage and children. Yes, she had planned their meeting, and accepted his invitation to dinner, and allowed this lovemaking which had left her so shaken and wild and restless. If on top of all this she suddenly asked him to father her child, how could she blame him if he grew suspicious about what else she might want from him?

And she wanted nothing else, nothing at all except perhaps sometimes his company for the child. Certainly not his money, and never, never marriage, not with him or anybody. But how to convince him of that?

She would just have to show him she wasn't the marrying kind. She climbed into bed and sat up among her pillows, wondering how she could set about it. Supposing she told him she had other men in her life? No, just telling wouldn't do, she'd have to act it.

She bit her lip with distaste, but forced herself to work through the idea. She would have to behave like a woman whose life was full of casual affairs, who was used to going from one bed to another, and who regarded this as only one adventure among many. For a while she'd have to assume a completely different personality, but she could do it if she tried. She'd start thinking herself into it right away.

'I'm hard,' she murmured aloud. 'I'm easy to get, but impossible to keep. Sexually, I'm the cat who walks by herself, and all men are alike to me.'

Put like that, it really didn't sound so bad. Thinking of the new landscapes, new seascapes, new pleasures she would soon be exploring with Bart, she slept till her alarm went off at seven.

Swaying on the train to Southampton next evening, she was astonished at how well everything had worked out. From first rising to pack, through the hectic office day preparing for her absence, to six o'clock when she had changed in the washroom to workmanlike jeans and stepped out of the building into the taxi she had ordered, everything had meshed like a well-oiled engine.

She had skipped lunch as usual, and not had time for supper, but that was all right. Last night's meal had stoked her up for days, and she was able to buy a black coffee on the train.

As she sipped, she couldn't stop herself counting every clack of the wheels. She tried to pretend it was sheer impatience to be on the water, but she couldn't fool herself. She knew exactly why her heart was hammering like this, and why it did flip-flops as Bart's lean figure, distinctive as ever in his usual blue-green shirt-jacket, sped towards her along the platform of Southampton station. She jumped down into his arms.

'Sensible clothes already?' He held her away for inspection. 'I hope you've got party gear in this bag as well.'

'I did pack a skirt and some tops,' she answered, content to be walled in again by his strength and his gentleness. 'The kind that double for sunbathing.'

'We'll certainly be doing that if the forecast's anything to go by.' He gestured with a wide sweep of his arm at the sunset sky. 'And we're going to see the New Forest at its best.'

He led her to a parked BMW. When he opened the back door for her bag, she saw one of the un-mistakable signs of the yachtsman: a pair of salt-stained wooden oars running lengthwise down the middle of the car, with the blades resting either side of the handbrake.

Settled beside him with the engine purring into life and the summer-evening city gliding by, she wondered how she would launch her new role. Somehow his big, warm presence, radiating con-fidence and capability, made it all more compli-cated than it had seemed in the small hours. Telling herself she mustn't start too soon, or be too heavy-handed about it, she shelved the question for the time being.

'I've never been to the New Forest. Is it nice?'

'It isn't Cornwall.'

She smiled at his patriotic caution. 'But apart from that?'

'Apart from that, yes, it is. Very nice.'

'Some might say,' she teased as leafy suburbs gave way to quiet villages, to dense-growing trees vivid with new leaves or to heathland rose-tinted by the sunset, 'it was even better.'

He grinned, and shrugged. 'They're entitled.'

'Such tolerance!'

'Oh, well. Not everybody's lucky enough to be Cornish.'

She chuckled and turned to him, 'Bart Rule, I do like you...' she began, and trailed off. Would the character she was playing speak or act as impulsively?

'Only like?' He was squinting sideways at her. 'That's what I call faint praise.'

'Not from me.' Telling herself it was now or never, she took a deep breath. 'And I reckon to know about these things.'

'What things?'

'Oh, you know. Men.'

He frowned slightly. 'Is that a boast or an apology?'

'I don't boast. Or apologise, for being... what I am.'

She watched him tensely, hoping she hadn't gone too far, and was annoyed to see she needn't have worried. His frown had given way to a rueful smile, and his hand reached out to close on hers.

'I'll tell you what you are, my love. You're tired, from all the hassle of getting here.'

'No, I'm not,' she answered sharply, and then, giving up for the time being, 'Well, maybe a bit.'

They made a brief pause in the lamp-gilded streets of Lymington. To Gemma's surprise a dark, middle-aged man greeted them from the pavement and let himself into their back seat.

'This is Mr Price, who helps look after Greatwoods,' Bart introduced him to Gemma. 'He'll be driving the car back there when we've finished with it.'

They continued out of town, presently nosing down a bumpy sideroad to an unlit strip of concrete surrounded by shingle.

'Where's the boat?' Gemma asked as she scrambled out. She could see lights and buildings some distance away, but no sign of life or even of water until the reedy wastes beyond the launching-strip.

'Patience.' Bart had lifted her bag from the car, and was now sliding the oars out one by one. 'It's low tide, I couldn't get the dinghy up here—as you see.' He indicated the dry shingle, and turned back to Mr Price who was already in the driving seat. 'That's it, then, and thanks. I'll be in touch.'

After some inaudible reply, the car backed and turned and drove away. Released from the dazzle of its headlights, Gemma found she could after all make out in the moonlight a few masts rising here and there among the reeds. Somewhere among the sea-noises came the muted flash of a lighthouse, so she supposed the open sea must be in that direction.

She held her arms close to her body, but couldn't stop the shiver that raised the hair on the back of her neck. She hadn't pictured anything quite so lonely. So cut off. She wished he hadn't sent the car away; it had suddenly come to seem like their one link with civilisation.

'There's a pub down the road, if you fancy a drink before we go on board.' His voice was reassuringly casual. 'Or would you rather wait, and have something hot from the galley?'

Soup! Her rebellious stomach sent the message into her mind so clearly, she could almost taste its life-giving savouriness.

'Some *bouillon* might be nice,' she said aloud, putting her hunger firmly in its place. 'Or hot lemon juice, if you have it.'

'Right, then, this way.' With the oars comfortably over one shoulder and her bag on the other, he set off across the shingle. 'I'd have brought a torch, but the moon's so bright.'

'I can see well enough, thank you.'

Concentrating on her balance among the smooth, loose stones, she didn't speak again. How lucky she'd known enough about the *Felicity*, and about small boats in general, to wear trainers from the start. She hadn't come expecting a glamorous cruise on a millionaire-style yacht, but even so she couldn't help feeling depressed. Surely there were easier ways of getting on board?

And it'll probably be horribly uncomfortable when we do reach it, she thought despondently. Men on their own never know how to look after themselves.

So the inflatable dinghy came as no surprise. She hated the way these things wrapped themselves round the water, but she did her best not to show it as she perched on its side. His oars propelled it into the hushed reeds so quietly that a pair of sleeping swans never lifted their tucked-back heads. She knew Bart liked places where he'd be left alone, but this was absurd, she thought grumpily. They were among moored boats now, but all were covered and silent. They might have been at the end of the world.

'Cheer up!' He rested the wet, gleaming oars and reached out to grip a white hull. Lightly balancing, he tied the dinghy to it, pushed the oars on board, and sent her bag after them before he turned back to her. 'Shall I go first to give you a hand?'

'I don't need a hand!' She shot upright, very much on her mettle. 'I've been messing about in boats since I was . . .'

She got no further. This cursed rubber contraption was quite different from the wooden boats she had grown up with, and responded to her sudden movement with a complicated dip which threw her wildly off balance. She was conscious of Bart's arm shooting out to steady her, but by the time he had grabbed her collar she was over the side and floundering in the freezing water.

It turned out to be only waist-deep, but that was the end of the good news. In spite of his steadying grip, she staggered and splashed as her feet sank into inches of oozing mud. When at last, clinging to Bart's hand, she came upright on the stones beneath the mud, her jeans clung wetly to her hips, her sweater released little runnels every time she moved, and her hair had turned to seaweed.

Still steadying her, Bart looked up at the *Felicity* then back to her predicament. Before she could stop him he had swung his legs over the side and slid into the water with her.

As if that would help, she thought in fury. When she realised his extra height and his controlled movements were keeping him completely dry above the waist, that only made it worse. Fuming, she felt herself swung up into his arms and found his mocking face close to hers.

'How long did you say you've been messing about in boats?'

'*B-boats.*' she gritted her teeth, but couldn't stop them chattering. 'Not b-b-blown-up p-p-prams...'

'Here,' he hoisted her to his shoulder, 'grab the deck-rail.'

She obeyed, streaming water and shivering worse than ever now she had left the warmth of his body.

'Right. Up you go.'

And up she went, raised by his hands under her rear until she could scramble over the rail. She hardly had time to hug herself and shiver again before he was with her, opening the main hatchway to the dark well of the cabin. He must have touched a switch too; white light blinked within and and settled to a cheerful radiance.

'Try not to fall down the steps.' He stood back for her. 'There are three of them.'

'I wouldn't...'

'Come on!'

She swung down the steps without another word, into a space that was surprisingly big and comfortable. Before she could take in more he was beside her, dropping her bag on a cushioned bench.

'Now, out of those wet clothes!'

He disappeared through a mahogany door at the far end. She thought he must have gone away to give her the privacy to change, but he emerged almost at once with a big towel, and took the sopping welt of her sweater in an impatient grip.

'Arms up,' he ordered, and pulled it over her head.

'You've got my T-shirt there as well,' she squeaked, temporarily blinded by dragging, wet folds.

'All the better. Come on, help me get you out of them.'

She raised her arms without further protest, and couldn't help sighing with relief as he freed her of the chilling wetness. Only when he had thrown sweater and T-shirt outside did she realise she was now naked to the waist. And far too blue and goose-bumpy to be at all seductive, she decided as she grabbed the towel.

'Sit down,' he commanded, and when she obeyed he unlaced her shoes and flung them after the rest of her clothes. 'I suppose you can take off your own pants?'

She huddled angrily into the towel. 'I could have taken off my own shoes, if you'd let me!'

'Get on with it, then.' He disappeared again through the door, but his voice goaded her from the other side of it. 'We're both dripping mud everywhere.'

It didn't improve her temper to find he was right; her feet were slithering in gritty ooze on the beautiful wood floor. When he returned, miraculously changed into dry trousers, she had made her muddy jeans into a pad and was dabbing at the smooth mahogany.

'No need for that.' He took them from her and put them with his own. 'We've got the right gear outside.'

He went out and dropped the muddy garments, then took a long-handled mop from somewhere and dipped it over the side. While he came back into the cabin and sluiced the floor, Gemma tucked her feet uneasily beneath her.

'Can I help?'

'Just sit there and keep out of trouble.'

She drew herself up with annoyance and nearly lost her towel. It was no use, all she could do was stay out of the way as he'd ordered, and be reluctantly impressed by his efficiency. Soon he had not only cleaned the floor but dried it too, and slung the mop outside before surveying her with something between pity and exasperation.

'Couldn't you at least have been drying your hair? Here,' he was suddenly at her side with another towel, 'let me do it.'

'Don't bother...'

Conscious of her nakedness, she tried to struggle away. He only came closer on the deep-padded bench, so close she could see each tiny bar of colour that went to make of the stripes of his turtle-neck shirt. Then he flung the towel over her head, and she was thankfully shut off from him.

She had to admit, it was comforting to be dried like this. She had forgotten how cold she was, until her tingling scalp reminded her of what it was like to be warm. He went on to deal with the length of her hair, cuddling her head against his chest as he folded the towel round strand after strand. The solidness of that broad chest under her cheek! The bliss of this glow which was spreading down her neck, over her shoulders and her breasts, opening a gushing spring within her.

You can't, she told herself, suddenly panic-stricken. And then, why not?

Very deliberately, she moved her shoulders the least little bit in their protecting towel. It draped more softly and one of her breasts peeped through the rough folds, the pink invitation of its tip clear for him to read.

If only he'd looked. But he didn't, he was still busy with her hair. She let the towel open further and nestled against him, bare toes seeking the top of his instep.

That did it. The contact sparked between them with numbing speed, and her hair settled wetly back to its full length as he dropped his towel to the couch.

'My sweet, you're still shivering.'

She licked her lips to make them shine. 'Not from cold.'

'I . . . see.'

His eyes flicked to her exposed breast. She took a sharp breath, as if his gaze alone was enough to start those multiple demands he so easily roused in her.

Remember your role, she told herself, and put a hand up to his cheek. The concealing towel slid away, and she let it go.

'You're very beautiful,' he murmured.

'You're not so bad yourself.' She raised her head to look him brazenly in the eyes. The tender grey gaze almost broke her resolution, but she stiffened and held on. 'Well?'

He looked back, a little puzzled.

'At a time like this,' she struggled to keep her voice hard and matter-of-fact, 'men don't usually just...talk to me.'

'They don't?'

His voice too had hardened. He raised his hands and played with her hungry breasts. She gasped, aware that other parts of her were was just as hungry, clamouring for his touch, whirling her again in that hot, invisible flood only he could stem.

Which was indeed what she was aiming for, but not quite yet. Not until she had hold of herself again. She mustn't, must not let herself be carried away like this, not till she had made sure he was quite clear on the kind of person she was meant to be.

She forced a taunting note into her voice. 'Is that all you can do?'

'What do you think?' he snapped, almost angry now.

'I think you might have a trick or two still to show me.'

'Like this, you mean?'

He went on tormenting one of her breasts while
he lowered his mouth to seize the other in his teeth.
For a moment she thought he would hurt her, but
he didn't, only held and nipped and moulded with
his tongue until she moaned aloud.

'Ah, don't! Don't!'

She clutched his hair but he stayed where he was,
did what she wanted. His mouth went to her other
breast, his hands smoothed their delightful, me-
andering way down to the narrowness of her waist,
the flatness of her belly, the outer hills and hollows
of each hip in turn, until she ceased to be a thinking
creature at all. Nothing mattered, nothing at all but
that inner flood which renewed itself wherever his
fingers strayed.

'Please, Bart!' Tuned and taut as a guitar string,
she reared back. 'Let me touch you.'

'Hm. I wonder.'

The cautious rebuff tore into her languor, and
her eyes flew open. His sideways, suspicious glance
was almost more than she could bear, but she told
herself it was exactly what she intended, and kept
her voice low and suggestive.

'Come on.' She reached out to the waistband of
his jeans. 'You've far too many clothes on.'

He still wanted her, she could tell that. His gaze
had fastened on her body again, and she saw he
was fascinated by the way her breasts, gathered between her extended arms, were thrusting their rosy
offerings forward to his feasting eyes. But when she
pulled at the catch of his jeans, he lifted her hand
firmly away.

'No, I'm not doing a striptease for you.'

The harshness of his tone made it a rebuke. Hurt and bewildered, she drew back and groped for the concealing refuge of her towel.

'And I suggest you go and put some clothes on.'

What would her new character have done now, the easy woman with her varied sexual enjoyments? Would she have flaunted herself anew, stroked and petted and enticed? Maybe, but Gemma didn't know how to do any of those things. She wasn't that woman, and for the moment, facing the hard, hooded glance, she was too chilled and unhappy to pretend any more.

'I'll get into my nightdress,' she muttered, shamefaced.

'Do that. And I'll show you your sleeping quarters.'

She jerked her head up to look at him. 'Aren't we even sharing a cabin?'

'I play these things by instinct,' he told her brutally. 'And for the moment, my instinct says no.'

Filled with weariness, she swallowed down the lump in her throat. What had she done to put him so horribly against her? Only offered herself to him for the kind of pleasure he must have known with dozens of women.

The white-lit cabin suddenly blurred, and she found her eyes being dabbed with a big handkerchief that smelt of outdoors.

'Th-thanks.' She let him dry her streaming cheeks. 'I d-don't know what's the matter with me...'

'It's late, and you're tired.' His tone had softened, and he pushed a draggled tress from her face. 'Let's get you to bed.'

She looked at each of his hands in turn. One held the handkerchief, the other had just drawn away from her hair as if it burnt him, and she knew he was keeping them well clear of trouble. Even so they were troubling enough, those hands, but she really couldn't cope with any more of that just now. She fixed her gaze on the neutral distance.

'I . . . I am tired.'

She realised with surprise that it was true. Now that she was admitting it, she could barely wrestle back the huge yawn trying to force itself over her tongue.

'Come on, I'll settle you down in the forecastle.'

'The *fo'csle*,' she pronounced it as he had done, following him with sleepy obedience through the mahogany door. 'Is that, sort of, the spare room?'

He chuckled. 'I haven't heard it called that before, but it'll do.'

'It certainly will,' she agreed. She had packed carefully, keeping in mind the possible shortage of space, but she saw now she would have plenty of room for all her gear in these mahogany cupboards; one of them even had a mirror and a shelf, as if meant to serve as a dressing-table. The two berths below the cupboards were wide and comfortable, a sleeping-bag spread on one with pillows in place and a little reading-light glowing.

He had put her bag on the other. She thought miserably of the nightdress she had folded at the top of it, white broderie anglaise which set off her tan and allowed tantalising, flattering glimpses of her body through its floating, flowing length. She might, after all, not have much use for that. It certainly wouldn't keep her warm.

'You're shivering again,' he observed. 'I'll get you a hot-water bottle.'

So this was what all her plans had come to: a hot-water bottle. 'No, thanks,' she muttered through her fatigue. 'I'm not quite an old lady yet.'

'You've had a ducking, though.' He took the rubber bottle from one of the cupboards. 'That's exactly the kind of accident I keep it for.'

He disappeared into the main cabin, and she searched her bag for the wretched nightdress. No, she couldn't bear the flimsy scrap; she dropped it and took out a pink knitted leisure-suit which covered her from neck to ankles.

Wearing that, she felt not only warmer but stronger. And the bottle was marvellous too when she had settled in the sleeping-bag and he had handed it to her.

'What a beautiful cover!' she exclaimed, holding it to the little reading light to examine the intricate interweave of lavender and grey.

'My...' He paused, as if coming to something he was reluctant to mention. Then he looked at her again, at the pink leisure-suit and the still-damp hair twisted for the night into spindly pigtails. 'My mother knitted it,' he went on. 'Cuddle it in now, and settle down.'

She obeyed, pushing it down to her feet and revelling in the warmth that stole out of it, closing her eyes to rest them...

'I didn't mean you go to go sleep that fast!'

His sharp voice roused her again, and she saw that he had seated himself on the other berth, well away from her.

'I haven't finished with you yet, Gemma Roseveare.'

She tucked the sleeping-bag up to her chin and watched him apprehensively from her pillow. What now? The small, golden light cast deep shadows in the hollows of his cheeks and the straight line of his jaw. He seemed hatchet-faced, dangerous almost—until he met her eyes, and the straight mouth softened.

'Well, I won't scold you any more tonight. We'll talk about it in the morning.'

'T-talk about what?'

'Never mind. Go to sleep.'

'How can I?' She hated the way she was sounding like a querulous little girl, but she had to know. 'When you say you're going to scold me some more in the morning?'

'I didn't say that.'

'Yes, you did,' she insisted. 'And I shan't sleep a wink until I know why you're cross with me.'

'I'm not cross with you.'

'Even if you aren't now, you were.' She gestured with her head towards the main cabin. 'Back there.'

He considered for a moment. 'All right, then, listen. Did you notice those swans among the reeds?'

She nodded on the pillow, seeing again the moon-silvered stillness of the swans asleep.

'I've always loved swans,' his voice was soft and caressing, his eyes sad, 'and not just because they're so beautiful. Have you noticed how they're always in pairs?'

She nodded. 'They mate for life.'

'Exactly. Now go to sleep.'

And she found she could. In some way she didn't understand, he had let her off the hook. Freed her to sleep in peace.

'Thank you, Bart.'

They were the last words she spoke that night. The brief touch of his lips on her cheek hardly disturbed her at all, and she never knew when he switched off the light.

CHAPTER SIX

SHE could feel the beat of his great wings, and her own were so weak, they would hardly lift her above the water. And now he had caught her in his arms, folded the white wings round their two bodies, swooped with her through wave after wave after wave...

Gemma woke reluctantly, wanting nothing but to be washed forever by those waves of sweetness. They died away and she opened her eyes to the muted dance of sunlight, bouncing up from the water and stippling her ceiling with darting shadows. She sighed and turned on her side, trying to work out what it all meant.

Bart was up, she could hear him moving about in the main cabin. It had been him in the dream, but he had also been a swan. Why a swan? What had put swans into her mind? She gave up the riddle as the mahogany door slid back.

'Hi. Would you like some coffee?'

She nodded, snuffing up the good, warm scent of it from the other cabin and opening heavy eyelids, but already he had gone. When he returned he came right in, hunched a little to squeeze his great height under the lower ceiling of this cabin. He hadn't done that last night, had he? Why not? she wondered blearily.

He was holding out a delicate porcelain mug fashioned so that it stood on its own stem and base. She wriggled up on her pillow to accept it with a murmur of thanks.

It only took one sip for the memory to sweep back in all its humiliation. She had offered herself to him, and he had rejected her. There had been something else too, some way in which he'd made it easier to bear. The idea of swans returned for a moment, but wouldn't make any sense and was soon lost again as she glanced up at him. He was thinking of the incident too, she saw it in the hooded eyes. They flicked over her leisure-suit, her lank hair half escaped from its pigtails, as if he were trying to put together a pattern and the pieces wouldn't fit.

'Th-thanks for the bottle,' she began nervously. 'I didn't expect to be so cold.'

His expression gave nothing away. 'It's always colder at sea.'

She wished he wouldn't loom over her like this, so uncomfortably stooped and yet so clearly not about to sit down. She knew now why he hadn't needed to stoop when he'd talked to her last night. It was because he *had* sat down, on the other berth, while he told her... whatever he'd told her. About swans.

'What time is it?'

He consulted the wide, practical dial of his gold watch. 'Twenty past eight.'

'So late?' She swallowed the last of her coffee. 'I didn't know I'd slept so long.'

'You'd had quite a day...' He paused, as if holding back from a difficult subject. 'I looked in when I first woke at seven,' he went on quickly, 'but you were still dead to the world, so I went ahead and showered.'

She picked up the subject with relief. 'You have a shower?'

'Come and see.'

It turned out that the panelled space between the cabins, which she had taken for a mere corridor, had a shower-stall on one side and a loo with a pull-down washbasin on the other.

'How clever!' She examined the thermostat. 'Hot water, too.'

'You could run the QE2 on the engine I've put in.' He looked at his watch again. 'Breakfast in ten minutes?'

'I'll be quicker than that.'

She finished her shower and shampoo in five. Back in her cabin to dress, she thought about the jungle-patterned shorts and suntop, but left them in favour of jeans and a long-sleeved white shirt, and caught her wet hair back in a coral-coloured scarf.

Bart, too, had been busy. A panelled section of the main cabin was slid back now to reveal a stove, cupboards, shelves, more of the bright mugs on hooks. More coffee was percolating, and the grill was lit with two plates warming beneath it. When Gemma appeared he drew out the grill-pan, revealing bacon browned and curling, exactly as she liked it.

'I've cooked enough of this for two.' He sliced tomatoes through their gleaming middles and laid them beside the bacon. 'But if you don't want any, I'll take it all and skip the eggs.'

'Have...' she licked her lips '...have you any muesli?'

He nodded towards the dining area she had hardly noticed last night. It was spread with a blue cloth and set with milk, butter, marmalade, all in dishes of the same fine porcelain as the mugs and plates which were also in place. The setting further from the stove had a spoon and bowl, and a packet of muesli.

She swallowed. 'Th-that'll do very well, thank you.'

'I thought it would.' He put the grill-pan back. 'I got it in specially for you.'

'Th-thanks,' she said without enthusiasm, and tried to think about something other than food. 'Where does my sleeping-bag go?'

He went on cutting bread in deft sweeps. 'You'll find plenty of room for it under your berth.'

Sure enough, she found the deep cushions of her berth could be propped back to reveal a lift-out panel and a lot of storage space beneath. She stowed her sleeping-bag and pillow and checked she had left everything tidy. Somehow, with Bart in this mood she wanted to keep on the right side of him.

'Open the forehatch,' he called from the cabin.

'The...'

'That skylight-thing in the ceiling. Let's have some air through before we set off.'

She identified the hatch and lifted it wide, soothed by the wavering shine of a blue-and-white morning on reedy water. Maybe she was wrong about Bart's mood. Maybe he just needed his breakfast. She had a mad idea of staying here until he had eaten, and the heartbreaking scent been carried away on the breeze.

Some hope. When she came back into the cabin, the hot savouriness came at her like a wave, this time with the extra tang of the tomatoes. It was more than a smell now, it was a perfume, a fragrance sweeter than roses as she took her place at the table.

Perhaps if she started her muesli? She put her hand on the packet, then looked again towards the stove. He was neatly lifting out the bacon and then, still shapely and barely seared by the heat, the tomatoes.

She noticed with a pang the way he kept his back turned. Had he really lost all interest in sharing meals with her? Certainly he wasn't about to waste any time this morning coaxing or teasing her about her diet. If she was to have any of that mouth-watering feast, she must make up her mind to ask for it herself, without any help from him.

It was the tomatoes, scarlet as sin, that settled it.

'C-can I . . .' it seemed to Gemma her voice came direct from her disobedient stomach, 'can I change my mind?'

'Very sensible,' he commented, unsmiling, and transferred half of what he had cooked to the other plate. 'It's a long crossing. Now, what about these eggs?'

They were free-range, the yolks proud and golden amid the perfectly crisped whites. They were the best eggs she had ever tasted, so good she used some of her bread to clean round the plate when she'd finished. After that, what with the butter and the marmalade, she didn't have any room for the muesli. It didn't matter, nothing mattered now that she felt so much stronger and the world was so much better a place.

She accepted another coffee, and sat over it, taking in for the first time the comforts of the *Felicity*. This hatch too was open, slid back to let in the sunny, gusty morning, the dry rustle of the reeds, the brightness of summer clouds curving in semicircles as the boat swung on its mooring.

Through the open roof and the blue-curtained windows, the patterns of sunlight shifted endlessly. First they would gleam on the meticulously clean stove, then dazzle from the stainless steel sink, then glow deep red from the mahogany worktops and cupboards. Heartened by her meal and able to chat about neutral things, Gemma indicated a cupboard with an outward-opening door.

'Why is that one different from the others?'

'It's my fridge.' Bart poured his own coffee. 'It goes on below the waterline, and I gave the door a double skin for insulation.'

'You thought it out for yourself, then?'

'I'd like a freezer,' he sipped his coffee, staring at the door and frowning, 'but I'm not sure if the battery will run it.'

'And you couldn't have a bigger battery?'

'I could, but that brings me back to the space problem.'

'But Bart . . .' She trailed off, puzzled at the way he was contriving for space he could have afforded twenty times over. 'Why not a bigger boat, then? In fact,' she went on, greatly daring, 'why not a sixty-footer, with a crew to look after it?'

He surveyed her, tense and alert. 'Would you prefer that?'

'No,' she answered in surprise, 'I like the *Felicity*.'

'And you don't mind the work?'

'Of course not, it's part of the fun. You promised,' she reminded him, 'to let me steer.'

He stirred and stirred at his coffee. 'So many people want to be waited on, and expect me to want the same.'

'I can see they'd have to think again about that.'

She found herself smiling at this new light on the problems of being rich and healthy, until she remembered his ex-wife. Presumably Caroline Lang liked to be waited on, and had done her best to organise them both accordingly.

'All the same,' she came back hastily to her earlier question, 'you surely don't need worry about space?'

'Yes, I do.' He sipped his coffee, back with the problem he had set himself. 'This is about as big as I can have it, for the price. Didn't you know?' he added as he saw her bewilderment. 'I'm making this to sell.'

'I see.' She observed the cabin with new eyes. 'It's a prototype, then?'

'And almost ready to go into production,' he agreed, responding to her genuine interest. 'I've bought a boatyard near home.' He paused, waiting for her to acknowledge the word.

She did, surprised to find how close his plans were to her own in respect. 'You mean Cornwall?'

'I'm moving to Pensilva Haven,' he confirmed. 'Once I've appointed agents, they can easily market this boat without me.'

'It's certainly very comfortable.'

'And a reasonable price for families to afford.'

'A family cruiser,' she murmured, understanding at last the reason for the unpretentious, tubby build of the *Felicity*. She remembered how he had told Jim Derby the boat worked a treat. So this was what he meant, that he was trying out his own design.

'It'll sleep five,' he told her with enthusiasm. 'Six, if most of them are kids. And it'll stand upright on a beach.'

She nodded, recalling the shallow water she had fallen into. 'And you don't need deep moorings, so it's safer.'

He agreed, pleased with her quick grasp of the essentials. 'I'm already starting the next prototype, but I want the *Felicity* to be my trademark. It means...' He stopped, as if regretting his excitement. 'Well, never mind that now.'

Chilled, she sought to regain the closeness of the last few minutes. 'Isn't this rather a change of rhythm for you? After electronics?'

'It's only going back to what I first wanted to do.' His tone remained cold. 'I trained for marine draughtsmanship at the Tech.'

'But you've come a long way since then.'

'And you knew it,' the storm-grey gaze flayed her like a whip, 'when you came to see me on Monday.'

She stiffened, suddenly cold in spite of the June sunshine. 'I think you'd better explain that.'

'And I think you understand me very well.'

She nodded, feeling a little sick. What a mess she'd made of this! She had staged her act, set out to show herself wanting nothing from him but a good time, and never once thought of the other conclusions he might draw from it. And he was so right. The woman she'd been playing last night could so easily have been after his money, too—what a fool she was not to have seen that! And how on earth was she going to convince him she wasn't?

The only thing to do was face it squarely, and try. 'You're talking about money, aren't you?' she demanded, cheeks flaming.

'It does have a way of getting into everything.'

She squirmed under his unwavering gaze. 'Not with me. If you think I'd ever, ever touch a penny of it, you don't know me at all.'

Perhaps her passionate conviction impressed him. His eyes were still watchful but less hard now, more puzzled, as they had been when he had wakened her this morning. He looked as if he couldn't make her out, and no wonder.

This, my girl, she told herself, is what you get when you try to play a part that doesn't suit you.

She sought desperately for more arguments. 'When I first saw you, you were dressed as you are now. Nobody's idea of a rich man.'

'You discovered I was, though,' he pointed out inexorably.

'I did, but...what can I say?' She spread her hands, helpless. 'Only that I don't care about your money. And I'd have to say that, whether it was true or not. Look,' she thought of another way to convince him, 'I enjoy my job, and it's well enough paid.'

'It has been known for jobs to go all the better with a little money to oil them.'

'Jobs in television, maybe...'

She caught herself back, confused anew. The last thing she wanted was to drag up his marriage.

'Exactly.' He had already pounced on her reference. 'We gave some fancy parties, Caroline and I, and they got her noticed.'

'But she was good,' Gemma floundered, desperate to get away from the unpleasant subject. 'In the end, that's what matters.'

'Yes, she was good. Is good.'

He sighed, and out of the blue it was with her again, this overwhelming desire to comfort him. To put her arms round him and kiss away the frown from between his brows, the lines that had suddenly etched themselves at the corners of his mouth. And she really couldn't, could not afford to feel like that about him. Especially now, when he believed she was mercenary. She distracted herself with an impatient shrug.

'None of this is getting me any nearer convincing you I'm not after your money.'

'Damn the wretched money. I'm half inclined to give it all away.' He turned on her again with that penetrating stare. 'Would you marry me if I were poor?'

'But that's just what I'm trying to tell you,' she shot at him triumphantly. 'I wouldn't marry you at all.' She saw from his sudden stillness that she had caught his attention, and hurried on, 'I wouldn't marry anybody. I just wouldn't marry. Period.'

'Point made.' The grating note was back in his voice. 'And I've seen what you do instead.'

She felt the heat rising to her cheeks again, but defended herself. 'It's not a crime for a woman to show she likes a man.'

'Or that she likes lots of men,' he snapped, tight-lipped.

So this was what happened when you played at being the hard-bitten sexual sophisticate. She supposed the kind of woman she had been trying to be would have laughed it off, called him a prude, perhaps even tempted him again. But she couldn't do any of those things. The cheap little phrases that would have served her purpose all stuck in her throat.

She started gathering the breakfast dishes to give herself something to do. 'Isn't it time we moved? The tide's dropping.'

He agreed impassively, and opened cupboards to show her where things went. She had an uneasy feeling he wasn't done with her yet, but at least he seemed to intend leaving the subject for the time being.

'You promised me some steering,' she reminded him.

He gestured at the piled dishes. 'As soon as you've done the washing up.'

'I see. So I'm stuck with the woman's work.'

He only shrugged, refusing to make an argument of it. 'I'll do it myself, if you'll start the engine and cast us off.'

'I could,' she retorted, 'if you'll show me how.'

'I will if you insist, but it'll delay us.' He glanced through the window at the patches of mud which were beginning to appear below the reeds. 'We might dry on, and have to wait twelve hours for next tide. Or is that what you had in mind?'

The grey eyes raked over her with a mixture of scorn and calculating desire. Feeling them stripping her for his pleasure, exactly as she had displayed herself to him last night, she shrank back into the modesty of her long-sleeved, high-necked shirt.

'I dare say,' he added as if enjoying her discomfort, 'you'll be glad to help me pass the time.'

She clenched her fists. 'I'll get on with the washing up.'

He turned away without another word and pressed a switch on the wall. The engine roared into life, and his next command had to be delivered in a raised voice over its steady chugging.

'When you've finished, you can come and take the helm while I hoist the sails.'

He swung up the steps, and she set about her task. After a moment, she realised she was positively enjoying it. Everything was so organised, the racks for crockery and cutlery so perfectly devised, she had no trouble guessing what belonged where. In fact, if he only kept his promise to let her steer, she could easily forget her problems and live for the moment. It was, after all, quite a moment.

When she presented herself on deck he quickly stood aside to hand over the wheel. From his watchful air, though, he wasn't taking anything for granted about her competence.

'Do you know port from starboard?'

'Really, Bart, I'm not a complete fool.'

'Which is which?' he persisted.

'When you're facing forward,' she said in resignation, 'port's on your left, starboard's your right.'

'Good, but let's just make sure. Show me the starboard side of the boat.'

She turned to look at him incredulously. 'You can't really believe I don't know my left from my right?'

'Mind your course,' he rapped out, 'unless you're planning to run us aground.'

She remembered how the *Felicity* would stay upright and comfortable out of the water, and bit her lip. Was there no end to the humiliation she'd brought on herself? Now he was hinting she'd strand them on purpose, so as to stay here alone with him until the next tide. She concentrated fiercely on holding the narrow, deep-water channel, conscious of his critical presence at her shoulder.

'Right, you can manage that bit,' he commented at last. 'Now let's settle the other thing. If I said pull to starboard, which way would you go?'

With a noisy sigh, she lifted her left hand from the wheel as an indication. She knew almost at once she had it wrong, and hastily changed it for the other, but the damage was done by then.

'You're putting me off,' she defended herself through gritted teeth. 'I couldn't have got to be a surveyor without a reasonably accurate sense of direction.'

'Reasonably accurate won't do,' he told her curtly. 'It has to be dead right.'

'It will be. Haven't you got some sails to hoist?'

'There's plenty of time.'

But as he spoke he was climbing easily to the cabin roof and making his way forward. In a few minutes the sails were up and filling, the boat leaping to the extra power so that she had to adjust her course to allow for it.

No wonder he'd managed such a quick getaway from those newsmen last Saturday. Was it really only last Saturday? Such a lot had happened since then. She'd made decisions which were going to change her whole life, and they'd all gone wrong, and now he hated her.

Well, she could at least show him she wasn't a complete parasite. If she worked hard now, made the best possible job of helping him as crew, he'd have to see her as a woman in her own right, not one who wanted propping up by any man, however rich. Setting herself to the steering with fresh resolution, she kept them to the very middle of the navigable channel, well away from the reedy shallows on either side.

He went below, and presently the rhythmic throbbing of the engine slowed and stopped. In the marvellous quiet she could hear the crunching hiss of their passage through the water, and the boat rose and leaned away from the wind.

They had almost reached open water. Guiding them towards it, Gemma suddenly felt all her worries and irritations driven out by a surge of well-being. It was such heaven to be here miles from anywhere, hanging as if on wings between sky and sea, hearing nothing but the call of the birds and the slap of the water, seeing nothing but blue sky and blue sea and blue land, white clouds and white sails and white boat . . .

'Starboard!' Bart called from below. 'Or were you planning to take the lighthouse with us?'

But his mockery was much less hurtful than his earlier sarcasm had been. It came out almost playfully, as if he too was elated to be under way. She was able to reply just as lightly.

'I dare say they want it left where it is.'

He came up, waving his old denim cap. 'With your permission?'

'Would it make any difference?'

She meant to be ironic, but her delight in being where she was, doing what she was doing, brought it out as mere teasing.

'I'm sorry you don't like it,' he adjusted it so that its peak shaded his eyes, 'but it *is* very comfortable.'

'A new one would be just as comfortable.'

'No, it wouldn't. A cap has to be broken in.'

'Well, that one certainly is broken.'

He settled on the broad bench with legs stretched along the deep cushions. His whole attitude was infused with placid ease, an acceptance as happy as her own of the moment for what it was.

'You're doing all right.' He surveyed the widening horizon, nose jutting from under the battered peak. 'Watch for bumpy water just here in the narrows.'

'Aye, aye, sir.'

The rough water closed round them and she revelled in the way they rode the shifting green translucence. It seemed to carry them along with it, out into the open sea where the water was much smoother, in spite of the brisk wind.

'We're moving nicely.' He nodded towards the south-west. 'See the Needles?'

She peered out at the huge white rocks with their red lighthouse, dramatically marking the western end of the Isle of Wight.

'They're more like teeth.'

'That's a matter of where you are. Wait till they're level.'

Sure enough, the rocks grew ever sharper as the boat rounded them. By the time they were dropping behind, Bart had fetched a heavy ship's compass from below, and set it into its bracket.

'Keep due south,' he ordered. 'I want to study the charts.'

She sketched a brisk salute, delighted to have proved he could trust her. While he went below and spread the table with charts, she held their course well clear of an oil tanker and two cross-Channel ferries. When he came on deck again, he actually smiled at her before he settled again with his feet up.

'If this suits you, it suits me,' he told her with a sigh, and leant back with his hat tipped over his eyes.

The Isle of Wight became blue and hazy with distance, the wind blew steady on the beam, and the sun climbed ever higher among the tufty clouds. They weren't exactly busy, indeed as the day grew warmer they had all the time in the world to chat of trivialities. But they couldn't have discussed anything serious, they were too interrupted by the busy traffic of the English Channel.

And there were so many small things to do. Bart changed into white bathing trunks, and Gemma, after a glance at his long, dark-tanned limbs, decided the sun was too good to be missed. So she gave up the wheel and put on the rejected shorts and top, twitching the narrow straps into place and trying not to be too self-conscious about the way the multi-coloured cotton wreathed her hips and breasts in exotic blooms.

He did give her one appreciative glance, but didn't comment. He didn't comment about her refusing to eat lunch either, which was just as well because she really couldn't have managed it after that breakfast. He ate bread and cheese himself, and then produced last night's wet clothes.

'I'd forgotten all about these.'

'Ugh.' She nudged the soggy bundle with her bare foot.

'They're all right, we'll rinse them in the sea.'

'You'll drop them overboard.'

'No, I won't.'

And he didn't. He trailed garment after garment out in the water, and hauled each one up to wring it and fasten it to the deck-rails. They hung, salt-streaked, in the lengthening rays of the sun, but at least they were free of mud.

'It's nice that the weather's staying with us,' he observed as the shadows lengthened. 'We'll be able to have supper on deck.'

'Supper?' She glanced with surprise at the French coast looming in the distance. 'I thought we'd be in harbour for that.'

He laughed as he went below. 'We'll be hours yet.'

She heard him moving about the cabin, and soon a rich medley of scents was spreading back to her from the stove. Something was simmering in wine, with a *bouquet garni*. And could that be bread baking? How had he managed to have bread baking, in five minutes?

'I didn't bake it, I got it in Lymington,' he corrected her as he set a tray on the deck and took over the steering. 'It's warmed up well, though.'

'It certainly has,' she answered through a mouthful. The long, gold-brown loaf was accompanied by beef in a thick sauce with tiny onions and mushrooms, set off perfectly by a shining green salad. 'Did you buy the stew, too?'

'*Boeuf bourguignon*, if you please,' he told her loftily. 'My party dish. I made it yesterday in your honour.'

She smiled, remembering the celery he'd been carrying when they first met. 'So you cook, too?'

'When I'm allowed,' he admitted. 'The house-keepers don't like me messing up their kitchens.'

'Do you mess them up?'

'Fair play, they have their job to do.'

Fair play. Gemma sat quiet, remembering all the people she knew who were fond of Bart. Jim Derby and Chief Hawkins were only the latest of them. Her home town was full of old schoolfriends, teachers, neighbours who spoke well of him, and one of the qualities she'd heard mentioned again and again was his sense of fair play. Yes, he always dealt fairly, that was one reason why he was so popular. One reason perhaps why she'd chosen him...

'There's a marina in Cherbourg,' his practical tone interrupted her thoughts, 'but it'll be late by the time we get in. What d'you think about anchoring for the night?'

'Whatever you say, Bart.'

She realised she really meant it. She knew she was safe with him; happy to do whatever he said. He would make the right decisions, for the right reasons, and whatever he decided was all right with her.

CHAPTER SEVEN

Bart told her that the outer harbour in Cherbourg, though enormous, was called the *Petite Rade*. Long before they reached it a waxy moon had risen above the darkening eastern rim, and the western sea glittered in a sunset delicate as the inside of a shell.

Gemma gave up the wheel and went forward to the prow just to revel in it. So when he asked her to look out for guidelights in the gathering darkness, she stayed where she was and called out instructions, happy that he trusted her to get it right, and that she was able to be so useful to him.

She never knew exactly when they entered the huge expanse of sheltered water. At some point he switched on the engine, and later shouted an order to release the anchor. She did, and felt the boat swing to a new rhythm as the anchor-chain tautened and the engine stilled. They had arrived.

'Sails!' shouted Bart.

They worked together by the boat's own lights and the white radiance of the moon to lower the great, flapping sails. It was a rewarding job. Each handled separate tasks, yet seemed to know by instinct what the other needed. In no time at all the sails were furled, and they were blinking and smiling at each other in the brightness of the cabin.

'That was a neat piece of teamwork,' he observed with satisfaction. 'We were right on the same wavelength.'

'It was marvellous!'

She breathed deep, revelling in his approval and in the achievement of a journey well finished. Better than that, in a sense stronger than she had ever experienced before of complete harmony with another human being.

Then, abruptly, it was all gone. The journey was over and the time of accounting had come. For the first time since he had put on the white trunks, she became aware of all the smooth length of him, each perfectly formed muscle rippling under the glossy skin. And her own suntop and shorts were suddenly far too brief. She knew he felt it too, she could tell by his quickened breathing and by the small, uncomfortable movement which took him a little away from her. It hurt, that movement, yet it was a relief too.

'I'm cold,' she lied. 'Could I borrow one of those beach robes from the fo'csle?'

'Help yourself.' His tone held all the harshness of last night's broken-off lovemaking, this morning's discord. 'And bring the other for me.'

When they were both covered from neck to knees in sea-blue towelling, she felt able to face him again. 'I know it's late,' she began hesitantly as she tied her girdle in place, 'but could we just sit on deck a little, now we're here?'

'Of course. Would you care for a drink before we turn in?'

Turn in where? she wondered, and had a bitter foreknowledge of the answer. From the way he had spoken, for all the world like a considerate host, she hadn't the slightest doubt that he meant them to have separate cabins again.

'Thanks, but I don't want anything. Except maybe,' she threw her head back to the night which lay silky and mysterious over the open hatch of their small, illuminated shell, 'to have the light out.'

He gave her a keen sideways look.

'It's such a beautiful night,' she explained hastily.

He flicked the switch. In the sudden dark she heard him move yet further away, mockingly bowing her up the steps. 'After you.'

She sighed, and went ahead of him to one of the deck benches. When he followed she wasn't at all surprised to see him take the other, as far away from her as he could politely get. He settled there in his favourite manner, back against the cabin wall and feet up, but she knew he was less relaxed than he looked.

However, when she tried the same posture on her own side she found it helped. Depression and nervousness started to drain out of her, out into the starlit grandeur where even the nearer boats seemed far-off as planets. The city glittered like a distant jewel, the water was tracked with gold and silver, the moon glowed high and pearly from opal clouds. She stole a glance at him, and saw that he too was enchanted.

'I've never seen it like this before.' He spoke softly into the hushed lapping of the water. 'It's quite something.'

'I wonder why a full moon is supposed to drive you out of your senses?' She spread her arms, letting the towelling sleeves drop back as if she were trying to soak up the peace-giving whiteness. 'It doesn't seem to affect me like that.'

'Doesn't it?' He sounded as if he really wanted to know, and surveyed her with an intentness which belied the indolent sprawl of his long limbs. 'Never at all?'

She stiffened, her calm invaded all over again. 'I don't know what you mean by that.'

'Yes, you do. For a while there, I thought I'd got the wrong woman.'

'Did you, indeed?' She bristled at his way of putting it. 'Well, you haven't *got* this woman at all.'

He turned his head lazily towards her. 'Some might take that as a challenge.'

'They'd soon find out different.'

'That's my Gemma.' He shot her a tormenting grin. 'Welcome back to the bossy little madam with the inflated ideas about herself.'

Speechless with indignation, she twisted to face him.

'Oh, some of them are justified,' he condescended to admit. 'You're pretty competent, when you're not showing off.'

'That's big of you.' She swung her feet to the deck and sprang up, glad to be looking down on him for once. 'And you, of course, are the perfect judge of competence.'

'Calm down, you'll have one of your accidents. Or maybe that's not such a bad idea.' He too swung his feet down, but stayed seated on the cushioned bench. 'Maybe this time I'll help it to happen.'

Before she knew what he was doing he had shot out a long arm and dragged her to his own bench with a mere two fingers thrust into her girdle. Its loose knot unravelled as she flopped down at his side, and she felt a button pop from her shorts.

'Get your hands off me,' she hissed in outrage.

But he didn't. Instead he set one on her waist, the other behind her shoulder, and drew her round to face him. Encircled, she fought the champagne tingle spreading through her blood from those two warm hands, muffled though they were by the towelling robe. She braced her arms against his chest.

'Please, Gemma.' He seemed scarcely to notice her struggles, his voice strangely detached compared to the urgency of his words. 'Let me touch you.'

She held him off in grim determination. The beach robe dropped from her shoulders and carried with it the narrow straps of her suntop, so that her thrust-forward breasts were almost exposed, but not quite, thank heaven. She knew how completely they would betray her. Under their thin covering of tropic-patterned cotton, the twin peaks had set up their demand the moment he touched her, but he wasn't going to see those if she could help it. Not like this.

'Is that all you can do?' Still using that oddly detached tone, he hardly seemed to be asking a question. 'I think you might have a trick or two still to show me.'

She froze, recognising the phrases at last. She had used them all herself last night, trying to goad and cajole him to casual, loveless coupling.

Before she could rally he had seized her in a hard, inescapable kiss. Excitement ran through her but she fought it and him, twisting in his grip, turning her head uselessly to free her mouth from his relentless lips and tongue. He let her go as suddenly as he had taken her and she flung back against the rail, panting.

'How...how *dare* you?' she raged as her breath came back. 'You...you were...'

'Come on, Gemma,' he taunted, not at all put out. 'Tell me what I was doing.'

'You were using me like an object!' she spat at him, enraged all the more by his persistent calm.

'Exactly as you invited me to do last night.'

The cool words dropped into her anger and brought her to a halt. She drew a trembling breath, trying to understand.

'And now we both know it's the last thing you want. So,' he went on, 'what were you up to last night?'

She gritted her teeth, seeing how he had tricked her. He'd taken her by surprise, deliberately forced her to fight him, and her struggles had completely given her away. The easy woman she had hoped to imitate would never have objected as she'd just done, and he knew it.

Fury welled up in her. All right, so he'd seen through her. But he hadn't been content with that, he'd had to devise a trap for her, manhandle her to make her betray herself. And he wasn't a bit ashamed of it, either. Whitened by the moonlight, he was all angles and contrasts, eyes shadowy, but mouth curving upwards—he was actually smiling.

'Oh, well. I suppose I'll find out some day why you tried to be a slut.'

'A *what*?' she gasped, more affronted than ever. 'Don't you dare use that word about me.'

'I didn't. I used it about what you were pretending to be.'

'It's still a beastly, sexist word.' She tried to conjure up the ideas she had used to talk herself into her role. 'I'm...I'm the cat who walks by herself.'

'But not the alley-cat,' he countered easily. 'I think we've settled that one for good and all.'

'Even alley-cats...' She broke off, realising she was accepting the word he had chosen, and corrected herself. 'Any woman has a right not to be mauled...'

She stopped, seeing the direction of his suddenly fascinated gaze, and found her indignation had completed the downfall of her suntop. She'd been so angry she hadn't noticed, but he had, and was reading the mute appeal of her breasts with complete accuracy. She hastily pulled the beach robe up over her shoulders, too embarrassed to care how the straps of the suntop beneath stayed uncomfortably over her arms and hampered her movements.

'Why bother to hide those now?' he demanded huskily. 'You've already made me a present of them.'

'That was...' She swallowed. 'That was when you were nice.'

'Nice!' He gave a throaty chuckle at the trite little word. 'Shall I be nice again, Gemma?'

'Get away from me!' She stood up hurriedly, and only then remembered the missing button on her shorts. She made a grab for them, but the straps of her suntop held her arms, the shorts slid to her hips, and the hasty movement entangled her in the trailing girdle of her beach robe. Before she knew what was happening she had sat down again, much closer to him, most of the beach robe bundled beneath her and no concealment for the two agitated crests, shamefully pink in the whiteness of the moon. She gasped, and put both hands up to cover them.

He repeated in that husky, teasing voice, 'Shall I be nice again, Gemma? Like this?'

His hand stole across her hips to the sea-green towelling and gently tugged at the crumpled folds she was sitting on. They resisted, and his hand rested on them feather-light while his other pulled both of hers gently away from her breasts. She closed her eyes and prepared herself for the honey and fire of his touch, but all he did was to pluck the towelling into place, covering her and keeping her covered. Only his knuckles brushed her, and that alone was enough to send the frustrated longing pulsing through every part of her body.

'If you'd ease up a minute,' he murmured. 'We could soon make you respectable.'

'No, you don't.' Encircled and enflamed, she turned away from him. 'You're not doing that to me again.'

'Doing what?' He pulled at the towelling, spreading new ripples of desire even as he carefully held away from her.

'P-putting me to bed with a hot-water bottle,' she gasped, unable for the life of her to make her voice come out normally.

He stopped pulling, and for a moment was completely still. Then he whispered into the moonlit solitude, 'Is that what you think I want to do, Gemma?'

'How do I know?' She kept her head turned away, unable to face him. 'You've badgered me until I don't know where I am.'

'Oh, my love!'

She jerked round to look at him, wide-eyed. 'D-do you really m-mean that?'

'My love, my love, my beautiful, silly, funny love,' he crooned. 'I love you, Gemma Roseveare.'

'B-but . . . you could have anybody.'

'I don't want just anybody. I never did. But I do want you.'

His hands released her, went to his own robe, opened it and let it fall to the cushion. Then he was out of his trunks in one lithe, silent movement which left him naked and vulnerable, his excitement as clear to her as hers had been to him.

'That's how it is with me, my darling.' He drew her to her feet. 'But it has to be love or nothing.'

'And with me, too,' she gasped, putting her hand out and daring to enjoy the smoothness of his shoulder. 'Only . . .'

'Only what, my love?' It came out muffled against her hair. He was all round her now, his arms, his lips, his hands working their sweet magic.

'Only, I never knew it before.'

His chest with its fine mat of hair, his belly flat and hard against hers, the beloved heat of his thighs, these were the world. She never knew how they got rid of her clothes, only that they were gone and that he was lifting her to the deck cushion. Then came an ecstasy almost beyond bearing, the waves of it constantly renewed until they reached the centre of her being and washed her into a unity with life itself, a oneness with all of this black and silver universe, from the sparkle of its stars to the power of the foaming sea beneath them.

'I never knew it could be like that,' she murmured drowsily, somewhere on the other side of that great wholeness. 'I don't believe I'll ever be just me by myself, ever again.'

When she next woke she wasn't on deck at all. It didn't matter because he was there too, snuggled up close on this huge divan-thing. She slept again, and it was morning.

'Bart,' she murmured into his ear, 'where are we?'

He stirred and kissed her neck. 'I don't know about you,' he murmured sleepily, 'but I'm in heaven.'

'But really, Bart, where are we?'

'You've forgotten?' He opened his eyes and lifted his head to survey her with a puzzled frown. 'We're on a boat, in Cherbourg,' he began very slowly and clearly. 'Do you know where Cherbourg is?'

'Silly!' She rubbed her finger along his jaw, loving its early-morning prickles. 'I mean, where on the *Felicity* is there a bed this big?'

'Oh, I see.' He closed his eyes again. 'It's the dining area. You lower the table and change the cushions.'

'It's lovely.' She settled back against him. 'I could stay here all day.'

He smoothed her thigh. 'Let's do that.'

A long time after, he showed her how to make the divan back into a table, and they had breakfast. Or something.

'Have we any shopping we should do?' she asked.

He shook his head. 'I stocked up in Lymington on Tuesday. We needn't go near the marina for days and days.'

She moved their plates to the sink with a chuckle. 'I begin to think you've something against the marina.'

'Only that it'll have lots of people about. Somehow,' the deep grey eyes met hers, 'I can't be doing with people, just now.'

'Oh, my darling!' she exclaimed, and forgot everything else for a while.

Only when he decided to eat toast did she remember what she had meant to ask. 'But don't you have to see somebody in Cherbourg?'

'Old Dumont?' He went on eating peacefully. 'No, he can look over the boat any time.'

'So you really are here on business?' She lowered her lashes. 'I thought you might be making that up to get me here.'

'I do have to appoint an agent.' His mouth quirked. 'But I took a few liberties with the timing. I've a week in hand.'

'Bart Rule!' She drew herself up in mock anger. 'You made me break the working habits of a lifetime...'

'They wanted breaking, you little workaholic.'

'Rushed me away at short notice...'

His hand closed over hers. 'Are you sorry?'

'What do you think?'

'I think,' he let go of her hand to reach for a chart, 'we might potter along the coast a bit. When we've time.'

As it turned out, they didn't for the rest of that day. What with finding their papers for the French police launch which came to inspect them, and leaning over the rail to watch a regatta, and going for a swim in the clear, deep water round the boat, and eating again late in the afternoon, the day was gone before they knew it. But the next day they managed to come down to earth a little earlier, and set a course through tossing white spume which carried them by evening to the tiny port of Barfleur.

The following day they went ashore there, and walked for miles along green Norman lanes, but neither Bart with his map nor Gemma with her surveyor's skills could have told their direction. They had supper in a quayside restaurant, but all Gemma could remember of it was accordion music and a quietly festive Saturday-night crowd. Even when Bart told her she had eaten pancakes with some kind of filling, she didn't think of her waistline.

The following day they made for St Vaast, and agreed it was the most delightful place in the world to eat oysters, and wondered if it was true about shellfish making you sexy.

Bart said firmly that it wasn't. 'Not for me. I've got you, what do I need with oysters?'

The June days slipped by like blue beads on a necklace. They laid in stocks of local cheese and pâté, and agreed that it was time to be right away from people again, so Bart pointed on the chart to the tiny Iles St Marcouf.

These turned out to be quite deserted. They rowed out the dinghy and pulled it up on the tiny shore of the biggest one to explore its massive, mysterious walls crumbling into decay and a ruined quay no boat could possibly reach any more. Then Gemma rowed them back to the *Felicity*, and Bart admitted she really didn't make a bad job of it.

The weather broke into thunderstorms next day so, as Bart pointed out, there was really no point in going on anywhere else.

'You're sure the anchor will hold?' she asked fearfully as the wind whirled them round and round on it.

'Like a rock,' he assured her.

It did, and the lightning and the thunder became part of a long, slow journey to pleasure. While she still clung to him, convinced that life could hold nothing better, he raised his head.

'Listen. The thunder's passed.'

'Mm,' she agreed sleepily. 'It's still raining, though.'

'Let's go on deck.'

'What, and be soaked?'

'We can soon dry ourselves. Come on.'

She followed him up the steps into a windy downpour that stung her body with a hundred rough caresses. The boat still whirled on its anchor and she clung to the rail, exhilarated by the noise and the movement of the tossing sea. He came behind her and she felt his excitement, shared it as he cupped her breasts and offered them to the endless dance of the raindrops until the tingling spread through her and she could bear it no longer. She turned to face him and was wrapped round once more by his warmth in the grey, blowing wilderness, wrapped and caught and held by heat and cold together until it all gathered and exploded into a new delight that left her weak and trembling.

'How did you know?' she asked afterwards, when they had showered and were drying themselves in the shelter of the cabin.

'I didn't,' he admitted, 'but it was fun finding out.'

'Everything's fun, with you. I wish I didn't have to be back at work on Monday.'

'And in Cherbourg tomorrow again,' he reminded her, 'if old Dumont's to look over the *Felicity*.'

'The *Happiness*,' she murmured. 'That's what the name means, isn't it?'

He nodded. 'And it's come truer than I ever hoped it could.'

'For me, too.'

She treasured her secret deep within her. Should she tell him? Not yet, she decided, not till he had asked her to marry him, and she had accepted. And maybe not even then, not till she knew for sure. It must have happened by now, so much ecstasy and such abandon could hardly have left her un-changed—but it could wait. There was plenty of time.

Thursday dawned blue and smiling as ever, and they set off again for Cherbourg. That evening they anchored again in the *Petite Rade*, ready for one last night alone together under the dwindling moon. A new heatwave had begun, and they sat on deck scantily clad and comfortable as Adam and Eve in Paradise.

'Happy?' He leant forward and stroked her instep.

'Happy,' she agreed, and sighed.

The next move must be his. All through this timeless interlude they had, as if by agreement, carefully avoided discussing what came next. Each moment had been enough in itself, offering so much to do, so much to see, so much to find out. So many small pleasures and great soul-shaking rhap-sodies—somehow, there hadn't been any time to talk.

But they must talk now. Or rather, he must speak, she couldn't do it for him. Her last words about their future had been seven days ago, when she had declared she wouldn't marry him or anybody. Could she perhaps help him by hinting how much she had changed her mind on that?

'Bart . . .'

'Gemma,' he spoke at exactly the same moment, and when she gestured him to go first, went on idly,

'I was just wondering if you were ready to explain the great alley-cat mystery.'

'Oh—that.' She sighed again. She must have been mad to think she would get away with that one, or even want to. 'Wasn't I an idiot?'

'What were you up to?'

'Oh, nothing.'

'Come on, Gemma.' He caught her reluctance and sat up, facing her. 'It's telling time.'

'It…it really wasn't anything.' She knew she was speaking too fast, but hurried on, 'I mean, I'm not like that, am I, and you know I'm not…'

'I do,' his eyes met hers, 'but I also need to know why you tried to be.'

'Does it matter?'

'A minute ago, I would have said no.' He held her eyes. 'Now I'm not so sure.'

'I promise I'll tell you soon.'

'So you *are* keeping something from me.' He was suddenly tense. 'I've always been straight with you, Gemma Roseveare. Now you've got to be straight with me.'

'I haven't *got to* do anything,' she contradicted him sharply.

'I see.' He never took his eyes off her. 'So this has been just a fling for you, after all?'

'No!' She too sat up. 'How can you say such a thing?'

'When I've as much riding on it as I have on this,' he replied doggedly, 'I'll say what I need to say. Now answer me. Are you serious about us?'

She met his eyes, not wanting to admit it, yet unable to back away from such an honest question.

'Yes, Bart,' she said at last.

'Right. Then I'm not having you hiding things from me.' He gripped her wrists and pulled her to her feet. 'I thought it was some silly joke, but it was more, wasn't it? You owe me the truth about it.'

'You'll get the truth.' She looked up, trying to stare him out. 'In my own good time.'

'I'll get it now. Or we're finished.'

'Bart!' She stared at him in astonishment. 'It's not that important.'

'Not yet. But it could be.' He let her go and gazed out across the dark water. 'I'm a one-woman man, Gemma. I married once, and thought I was settled for life.' He sighed, and turned back to her. 'Nothing's sure in this world, but that isn't going to stop me being damned careful before I marry again.'

'I see.'

She wanted to be angry with him, to regard these persistent questions as an invasion of her privacy, but she couldn't. His lost, vulnerable expression was too much for her. She was almost sure now that his first marriage and its break-up had somehow hurt him badly. Now that they were at last forgetting passion to talk seriously, he would probably tell her about it.

All the same, she had to protest. 'I can't believe that what we've been to each other these past few days goes for nothing.'

'It couldn't. But it'll never grow into anything more, either, unless I know I can trust you.'

She saw that he meant it, and perhaps he was right. At any rate, he intended to know her secret. And really, it wasn't so very secret. He'd find out anyway in the fullness of time. She took a deep breath, sought for the right words, and decided the only thing to do was get through it fast.

'I acted like that because I decided to try and have a baby. I chose you to be the father.'

CHAPTER EIGHT

THE WORDS dropped into a silence that went on and on. Gemma heard again the water lapping and hissing, the soft breeze tapping the rigging against the mast. She was glad of that breeze, grateful for the way it lifted the fine hairs from her forehead and cooled the sudden heat she could feel in her cheeks. And still Bart didn't speak, didn't move, didn't alter the pattern of his breathing. He was staring at her with a slight frown, his tongue just visible between his lips as if he were chewing on it in thought. He met her questioning gaze and spoke slowly, heavy eyebrows together.

'Let me get this clear. You wanted me to make you pregnant.'

She nodded, suddenly breathless.

'And the alley-cat act was to encourage me not to take you seriously,' he went on with reluctant anger, as if his worst fears had been confirmed, 'leaving the field clear for you and your baby.'

'It's—it's often done nowadays.' She knew she sounded as if she were justifying herself, and tried to be more assured. 'Women with careers don't always need . . . don't always want . . .'

'. . . to be bothered with a man in their lives,' he finished the idea for her, and stood up abruptly. 'I think,' he said in a tone she hardly recognised, 'you'd better turn in.'

133

'But . . .'

'Or let me put it another way.' He whirled from her with sudden savagery. 'Get out of my sight.'

Almost before she knew it she had risen and gone below. Only in the warm darkness of the cabin, listening to his brisk footsteps on the deck above, did she stop to wonder why she'd obeyed so promptly. Was it that she'd suddenly been afraid? Or even . . . ashamed?

Certainly not, she told herself, she'd done nothing to be ashamed of. If she had made him angry, that was his problem, not hers. She needn't feel so lonely, so lost, so empty suddenly in the dark well of this boat which had held so much happiness.

Now what was he doing? She peered out, just in time to see him spring to the rail and over it, stand outlined in perfect manhood against the moonlight with arms raised, and launch himself at exactly the right angle to part the water with hardly a splash. When she rushed to the side he was swimming vigorously away from the boat.

'What's got into you?' Her shout was a mere thread in the black and silver hugeness of sea and sky.

He didn't answer, just turned over and kicked up a lacy cascade of splashes before he headed back to the boat. Soon he was circling it one way and then the other, kicking again, playing in the water where they had once played together. Giving up in disgust, she went below and switched on the cabin light. By the time he climbed back on board she had filled the kettle and brought it to the boil. She was also rather on the boil herself.

'Robe!' he called from the deck.

She thought of telling him to fetch it himself, but quailed. She hadn't seen him like this since the start of the voyage, but she remembered that well enough to fetch his robe and throw it out to him as he'd demanded. When he came in with it fastened tight round him, she nodded at the kettle.

'I thought you might like a hot drink.'

'Wrong again.' With chilly good humour he took a bottle from the cupboard and one glass from its clip. 'I'm having a whisky.'

'You wouldn't think of offering me one?'

She watched him silently measuring whisky, and in spite of her respect for his temper, her own flared. Almost, he might have been dismissing her as not worth answering. When he had done with the bottle, he pushed it at her.

'Take what you want.' Still coldly equable, he splashed water into his glass. 'You will, anyway. I gather it's how you run your life.'

'That's not fair...' She stopped, appalled at the thin, pleading note in her voice.

'Isn't it?' He sat on the other side of the table, far away from her. 'I rather think we're back where we came in.'

'What do you mean by that?'

'Money.' He sipped the whisky, rolled it round his tongue, swallowed it. His eyes flicked over hers, the merest fraction less cold as they took in her bewilderment. 'There are things called paternity suits,' he explained briefly.

This was getting worse and worse. 'I...' She gulped, and went on, 'I'd never dream of anything so sordid.'

'No? And it isn't sordid to trick me into fathering your child?'

'No!' she responded angrily. 'That is, I didn't...I haven't... Oh, Bart, I don't even know if I've managed it yet.'

'But you've had a damned good try.'

'All right.' Close to tears, she faced him at last. 'But anyway, it wasn't for money.'

He leant forward and studied her intently in the hard overhead light. 'You know, I think I believe you.' He sounded detached, even a little amused, 'So you really meant it when you said you didn't want money from me?'

'None you don't want to give. Of course,' she seized the chance to expound at last, 'I'd have wanted you to know him.'

'Him?'

'Or her. But boys need a role-model...' She trailed off, her words shrinking to mere jargon as she saw his contempt.

'And girls don't need a father?'

His voice was still level, yet every word pierced. She thought of her own father's loving kindness, the jokes he shared with his daughters, the glimpses he had given them of a piquantly different, masculine world. Once more she was ashamed, yet surely not all fathers were as good as hers? And anyway...

'Fathers can be done without,' she mumbled to the table.

'Not entirely,' he corrected her with dangerous mildness. 'Even artificial insemination needs a donor.'

'Bart, how can you . . .'

'Mr Rule,' he rapped out, 'to you.'

Dismayed, she stared across the table at what had become an impassive stranger. This must be how the business world saw him: alert, guarded, unyielding as stone beneath the smooth surface.

'Shall I tell you why I swam just now?' he went on, quiet as ever. 'It was because I needed to do something energetic. To cool off, so I wouldn't hurt you.'

She gazed at him, wide-eyed. 'You wouldn't have? Not really?'

'You'd better believe me, Miss Roseveare,' he saw her flinch at the formality, and smiled mockingly, 'I would most definitely have hurt you. Then I'd have,' he paused, choosing the word, 'enjoyed you, and probably hurt you more.'

She was silenced as she took in the ugly picture. He'd been so angry with her, he'd wanted to use sex to punish her.

'Though I don't suppose you'd have minded that,' he ground on. 'It's a small enough price to pay for free treatment.'

'Bart!'

'But as far as I'm concerned, Miss Roseveare, the course is over.'

She swallowed hard and clenched her fists, forcing herself to speak calmly. 'You're being completely unreasonable. All I did was pay you the compliment . . .'

'Compliment!' he burst out, and let the word hang in the air while he drained his whisky.

Compliment, *compliment*, *compliment*, the anchor-chain creaked as the boat swung round in the wind.

'Maybe I'm just old-fashioned,' he went on more quietly as he put down his glass. 'Remember the days when a man mustn't want a woman only for her body?'

She stared at him. 'What are you talking about?'

'This *compliment*. What it amounted to was, you didn't want me, only my...'

'You've no right to say that,' she cut in, hating the way he was cheapening all her hopes and plans. 'I...I *chose* you.'

'Only, you forgot to take this into account. If I'd known what you were doing, I'd never, never have chosen *you*.'

'I see.' She shivered in the mild air.

'You understand? Never. Never!' The whisky-glass danced as he thumped the table. 'My children are going to have a *father*.' He shot the word at her with scalding contempt. 'Not be forced to make do with a cold-hearted, cold-blooded, half-baked career woman.'

'You say that as if it were a crime to be a career woman!'

'Not at all. But it *is* a crime to...' He sought for words, and gave up in disgust. 'You're no more fit to be a mother than you are to be a wife.'

She froze, paralysed by the finality of it, and he went straight to practical details.

'You do know, I suppose, that babies aren't just cute little bundles? That they have to fed, and kept clean?'

'What do you take me for?' she defended herself. 'I had it all worked out.'

'Don't tell me. You'll have a child-minder.'

'There's nothing wrong with that.'

'Poor little object. No brothers or sisters...unless,' the thick eyebrows took on an ironic slant, 'you were planning to do some more of this?'

'Of course not...' she snapped out, and then, squirming in the harshness of his condemnation, 'B-being an o-only child isn't that bad.'

'No brothers or sisters,' he repeated in a tone that showed his worst fears confirmed. 'And no father.'

'I told you I wanted it to be friends with its father.'

'No father,' he went on implacably, 'and a mother who calls her son or daughter,' his mouth turned down in disgust, '*it*.'

'That's only because I don't know yet which it's to be.'

'A mother,' he rode down her protests, 'who hasn't the first idea what she's doing.'

His deep voice thundered to a halt, leaving wave-washed silence behind it. Gemma was as angry as he was, yet when she eventually made her protest it sounded thin and choked.

'You...you've no right to say that.'

'And you've no right to treat a child like a...like a new car,' he answered more quietly, 'or a country cottage. A bit inconvenient, a bit expensive, but worth owning if you're prepared to put yourself out.'

'It's not like that at all.'

'No?' He stood up, yawning. 'I think we'd better go to bed. It's been a long day.'

'But...but you can't just leave it there! You haven't let me put my side at all...'

'You mean you can make it sound better?'

'It's every woman's right to have a child if she wants.'

'Spare me the women's rights bit,' he turned away in disgust and began to wash his glass, 'What about the child's right to be born of a loving partnership?'

'Partnerships break up.' She raised her voice to be heard above the noise of water in the sink. 'Partners often end by hating each other...'

'And you thought we would?' The noise stopped abruptly as he whirled to face her.

She hesitated, distracted by his height and fierceness. 'I didn't say that. I was just making a point.'

'You're no more committed to me now than you were at the start,' he tore through her protest. 'You've been using me, Gemma Roseveare, and I'll never forgive you for that.'

Shouted down again, she sat for a moment, stiff with fury and misery. This was getting her no-where—he just felt too strongly on the subject to make sense. Somewhere beyond their little fibreglass shell a bigger boat chugged by, its noise receding and its wake bobbing them gently back and forth for a moment or two. She felt it pushing her into her corner, and took a deep breath.

'I think I'd better find a hotel for the night.'

'Don't be silly.' He disappeared into the fore-castle and his voice came out of it, preoccupied, as if he were busy with some small task. 'Or are you going to walk on the water?'

'I can row...'

'Help yourself, then.' He emerged with his sleeping-bag and pillow, and jerked his head behind him to the forecastle. 'The dinghy's in its bag.'

'But...if I take it, how will you get ashore later?'

'You forget, I'm going to the marina tomorrow. If you hand over the dingy there, I'll pick it up.'

She realised he was calling her bluff, forcing her to be as self-sufficient as she'd said she could be. Miserably she contemplated what it would involve. She'd have to lug the dinghy on deck, inflate it, and row it goodness knew how far in the dark through the unknown hazards of a city harbour. Then she'd have to hand it over as he'd instructed, which meant finding the marina and making herself understood in French to whoever was in charge of it. Then she could start looking for a hotel.

'Right,' she snapped. 'I'll stay till we get to the marina.'

And that was it. End of conversation. He arranged his sleeping-bag and pillow along the quarterberth, finished washing his glass, and put it and the bottle away. Then he turned to her with cold courtesy.

'Your bed's made.'

'If you mean you want to be rid of me from this cabin...'

'Not at all,' he responded as if to a stranger. 'You're still my guest.'

'Your *guest*!'

'Until the morning,' he raised his voice over her interruption, 'but I think we'd be wise to try and sleep now.'

And somehow, a suggestion from Bart still had the force of an order. Besides, what else was there to do? She couldn't make him see sense if he wouldn't even listen, and as he'd pointed out, they did need to sleep.

Only, she couldn't. She turned again and again in her berth, unzipped the sleeping-bag to cool herself, and tried desperately to stave off yet another replay of the wretched, futile argument.

She'd think about where she went from here. She'd show him! She wouldn't go home, not when she still had a weekend of holiday left, but she'd pack her bag, and when they reached the marina would simply jump down to the pontoon and walk away.

Then she'd find a hotel, and explore Cherbourg. Alone. And not allow herself a minute to consider why it should now seem such a dismal prospect, when she'd been so looking forward to it. Yes, she would visit the botanical gardens, walk up the Roule for the view, she could do it all just as well by herself. And she didn't have to eat at the Cerf, where Bart had promised her the best sole *Normande* in the western world. A person could live without the best sole *Normande* in the western world.

It would do her good to be alone and unoccupied for a while. She'd have time to consider, draw up a short list perhaps of men who could be asked... who could be paid the compliment...

The compliment, the compliment, the compliment, the gulls screamed overhead as they scavenged for their first meal of the day. Gemma made one last effort to relax, turning on her back and consciously clenching and loosening each set of muscles in turn. It was useless, though; she knew now without a shadow of doubt what a fool she was. Whatever had come over her, what spirit of contrariness had possessed her at the start of this adventure, to keep from her the knowledge that it wasn't just Bart's child she wanted, but Bart himself? Wanted him with a longing which, now she had lost him, was almost too great to be borne. Wanted him to have and to hold, from this day forward, until death...

Only it would never have been possible, would it? The stupid man was a mass of prejudices—hated estate agents, hated career women, hated the thought of her having his child without him...

And so do I, she admitted to herself.

After that, a series of wretched pictures came to plague her. Of a maternity ward at visiting time with no Bart beside her; of a beloved child's first words, first steps, with no Bart to share her joy in them; of childish illnesses, accidents, arguments, with no Bart to support her through the fatigue and worry and wondering.

I may or may not have the baby, she thought bitterly, but I've thrown away everything else.

Somewhere far away, she was aware of noises. A deep, rhythmic thud started up, quite restful in its regularity, then rattlings on the deck above her, and a different feel to the motion of the boat. It didn't matter, she knew she was safe with Bart. The regular beat stopped and let smaller sounds through, the metallic tap of rigging against masts, footsteps, voices...

Voices? She opened her eyes, sat up, pulled the curtain back from her tiny window. Only yards away loomed the smart orange hull of another boat, right alongside, blocking out everything else, and the footsteps were on the pontoon. It was half-past nine, and they were in the marina. Could she really have slept through the raising of the anchor, the starting of the engine, the motoring through the harbour? She threw on her clothes and went into the cabin, which was rich with the scent of fresh coffee and wide open to another brilliant day.

'So you're awake.' Bart came in from the deck, and at once the cabin seemed narrow and confined in a way it never had before. 'I'll get breakfast.'

'Don't bother on my account.'

His lips tightened as if to hold back what he might have said. 'Suit yourself. Coffee?'

'Thanks, I'll get my own.'

She lifted the percolator. Somehow it managed to pour crooked and slop over, but as soon as she'd replaced it on the stove she wiped her mug, and the worktop. Then she doggedly rinsed the dishcloth.

'D'you have to fuss like that?'

Startled, she turned to look up into eyes whose sea-grey had hardened to ice. She tightened her lips. 'I'm leaving this galley as I'd wish to find it . . .'

'You sound like a notice in a public loo.' He moved towards her, reaching for the percolator. 'D'you ever do any thinking for yourself, or is it all slogans and catch-phrases?'

'You've . . . you've no right to say that . . .' She broke off to slide behind the table and make way for him, quite without her conscious will or consent.

'We're on rights again, are we?' He filled a mug for himself. 'You women whinge on a lot about those, don't you?' he added as he took the bench at the other side of the table.

She hastily drew her feet away from any accidental contact, and sipped her coffee. Feeling the strength of it flowing through her, she decided that if he wanted a fight she'd give him one, and cupped her hands round the mug while she drew in a deep breath.

'It depends what kind of man we're with,' she told him in a tone of acid, controlled sweetness.

'Does it hell!' he snorted. 'You know damn well women aren't that sensible.'

'I can see you're an expert.'

'They go by the moon, the weather, what they had for breakfast, whatever they've taken into their heads . . .'

'I'm surprised you ever let us have the vote,' she spat, outraged at this picture of flighty, frivolous womanhood. 'Whimsical little things like us.'

'The vote's one thing. Grabbing everything you want like a monkey, that's something else.'

'I see. We should leave that to the men, should we?'

He drained his coffee and banged down the mug. 'Men don't have babies...'

'And women shouldn't have anything else. I'm glad I've found you out, Bart Rule.'

'*You're* glad? What about the lucky escape *I've* had?'

'And just what d'you think you've escaped from?' she demanded in a fury. 'A serious relationship with me? Because if I was ever going to...'

'Here we go again. *A serious relationship*,' he mimicked her in a solemn falsetto. 'Why can't you forget the gobbledegook and use words that mean something?'

'I will! You're the worst male chauvinist...' She stopped, speechless with fury as she realised he was speaking in chorus with her, knowing exactly what she was going to say.

'...*pig I ever met,*' he finished for her in his mocking falsetto. 'And you call that meaning something?'

'You're right, I shouldn't say that. I've always had some respect for pigs.' She leant forward, hands stiff on the table. 'They're clever, lovable creatures compared with men like you.'

'Some straight talk at last.' He gave her a slow handclap. 'See if you can keep it up now, and tell me about men like me.'

'They're not very interesting, and neither are you.'

'But you're still going to tell me.'

'Men like you,' she persisted, refusing to let his mockery put her off, 'just have to be boss. Can't let women run their own lives.'

'That's rubbish and you know it!' He banged down his mug. 'It's not your life we're talking about, it's someone else's, a child's.'

'And you can't bear the thought of a woman taking that responsibility on herself, can you?'

Her misery of last night rose in her mind as she spoke, but she brushed it aside. So the small hours had given her a glimpse of the loneliness of single parenthood—she wasn't going to let herself remember that now, when he was behaving so abominably.

'It just doesn't fit into your world, does it?' she went on, as much for her own benefit as his. 'Women relying on themselves, making their own decisions...'

'You're forgetting, this particular *decision*,' his distasteful emphasis made it clear it was her word, not his, 'could hardly have gone ahead without my co-operation.'

'Yes, it could,' she contradicted him recklessly. 'It only needed one thing from you—and up to last night, you were happy to supply it.'

His thick eyebrows drew together. 'Are you saying...'

'You know good and well what I'm saying. You might think I was *using* you,' she threw his own word back at him, 'but I hope you're not going to deny you enjoyed it.'

'As if that kind of enjoyment mattered a damn!'

'Don't,' she choked, stricken by a sudden, vivid memory of the sweetness of his hands and his mouth. 'Don't cheapen it like that.'

'You're the one who's cheapened it. For good and all.'

'I didn't!'

'You let me serve you like a stallion does a mare. Like a ram does a ewe. Like a dog does...'

'Stop it!' She put her hands over her ears and closed her eyes, unable to bear any more of his relentless farmyard images. 'That's a foul way of putting it.'

'It's a foul thing to have done.'

'It is not!'

She opened her eyes, and a new tide of rage washed over her. He might have upset her, but he hadn't silenced her. She faced him anew, determined to pierce his guard as he had pierced hers.

'You're just being horrid...' Conscious of sounding like a spoilt little girl, she quickly chose another way of putting it, 'I mean, offensive, because you don't like having to see somebody else's point of view.'

'I certainly don't like hearing the facts twisted.'

'So I'm twisting the facts, am I?' She glared at him. 'Try this twist, then. You were happy to make love to me as long as you got all your own way.'

'And what, in your opinion, is my way?'

'I don't know,' she said wildly. 'I'm only just beginning to find you out.'

'And knowing so little about me, you still wanted a child by me?'

'I must have been mad.'

His eyes met hers, chill as a winter wind in spite of his smile and his mock-courteous bow across the table. 'Snap.'

She hardly heard him. 'I certainly couldn't live with you, ever, ever, ever...'

'It's manners to wait till you're asked.' His deep voice imposed itself on her this time without effort.

'Oh, you...'

She clenched her fists and leant towards him, breathing hard. He was so big, so relaxed, so very much getting the better of her without trying—would nothing reach him? She cast round for the worst weapon she could think of.

'I can see why your wife left you...'

That had done it. He drew a sharp breath. 'Be careful.'

She charged on, too triumphant to heed the warning. 'I suppose she put up with you as long as she could...'

'Be careful, I said.'

His voice dropped to a menacing hiss which commanded her attention in spite of herself. For the first time since he'd made her so angry she really looked at him, and couldn't help a shiver going down her spine. This was how he'd been last night before he went swimming, only she was nearer this time and could see the stony cast of his features, the lines etched round his nostrils, the suddenly prominent pulse beating in his temple.

Well, she wasn't backing off now. 'But she was bound to want a life of her own at last...'

'Third warning, Gemma.'

He had half risen now and was towering over her, voice dangerously low. She blinked up at him and held his gaze, refusing to be stared down. Just because he was stronger, he needn't think he was going to intimidate her.

'Yes, I can see you don't like talking about it,' she pressed on. 'It must have been a barren affair, your marriage...'

She broke off with a gasp. His hand had shot out, the slap catching her full on the cheek and the noise of it exploding in her ears as she rocked back in her seat. Tears sprang to her eyes from the shock, yet even while her own hand rose to her burning cheek she was conscious that it had only been a light blow.

He must have held himself back from really hurting her, and somehow that made it all the worse. As long as he was pulling his punches he was still in command, still winning. She'd been fighting him every way she could, no holds barred, had provoked him enough to hit her—and still he'd used no more force than he'd needed to stop her talking. To stop her impertinent comments on his marriage, which was none of her business.

Yes, he'd known exactly what he was doing, and he'd won. Brought to a full stop by the sting in her cheek, she could see now exactly how outrageous she'd been. How stupidly intrusive, how out of line, above all how...

How small. She'd gone for him like a little yappy cur, harassing and snapping until finally she'd become too tiresome and, like a bored mastiff, he'd given her just one nip to shut her up.

All the same, to hit her! 'Nobody's ever done that to me before,' she hissed through lips grown stiff with chagrin.

'Somebody should have.' He was perfectly quiet and relaxed again. 'Your parents have a lot to answer for...'

'Stick to the point!'

'They are the point.' His deep voice rode her interruption without effort. 'Unless it's somebody else who's spoilt you.'

'They certainly wouldn't ever have hit me...' She trailed off, reminded of her adoring parents, and dear Tamsin who had inherited their good nature. For the first time in her life it occurred to her to wonder if, in such an easy-going family, she'd had more of her own way than was good for her.

But that was exactly what he wanted her to think. She took her hand from her cheek, where the sting was already fading, and folded it with the other on the table to rally herself.

'Violence is never the answer.'

'We're back to the slogans, are we?'

He was looking out of the window in an elaborate charade of boredom. Or maybe, she thought with a sinking heart, maybe he really was bored. He'd dealt with the spoilt little girl, taught the yappy cur a lesson—maybe he now wanted nothing but to be left in peace to get on with his business dealings.

Sure enough, he was looking at his watch. 'We'd better think about putting you on a ferry.'

It was exactly the way he'd dismissed her last night, brisk and practical, making the best of a bad job. Only this time it was final. He wanted to be rid of her for good. She felt her scalp prickle with mortification as she realised how she'd outstayed her welcome.

'I ... I'm not going back to England straight away,' she muttered. 'Now I'm here in France I might as well enjoy it ...'

Enjoy it—what a hollow ring that had! To cover her misery she slid hastily out of her corner and stumbled into the forecastle to pack. It ought to have been a short job, but she couldn't even begin until she had rolled up her sleeping-bag, and the wretched thing seemed determined to escape her whatever she did. He wasn't making it any easier either by lounging in the doorway, surveying her efforts with a sardonic smile.

'Let me do that.'

'I'll manage.' She made another assault on the slippery nylon.

'I'll have to wash it, anyway.' He took it from her and disappeared into the cabin.

Presumably he was stowing her sleeping-bag somewhere out of his way until he could remove from it, as from the rest of the boat, all traces of her presence. Yes, that was exactly what he must be doing; his voice sounded preoccupied as he called back through the doorway.

'Do you know which hotel you're going to?'

She folded the leisure-suit she'd never worn since that first night, and stuffed it into her holdall. 'I'll find somewhere.'

'I'll take you to the Clermont.'

'No need, thank you.'

She gathered her toothbrush from the washplace and checked for anything she'd forgotten. Then she zipped her bag and hauled it awkwardly into the cabin. She was determined to refuse all offers of help, but when she found the cabin empty with that tidy, definite emptiness which said it was about to be left locked, she couldn't resist a surge of hope.

If he really did mean to escort her to a hotel she couldn't stop him, could she? And if he did that— the thought came to her unbidden as she heaved the bag up the steps to the cockpit—if he did that, he would know where she was. Would be able to find her if he wanted her again...

The hope died the moment she saw him. Feet up, plaited straw shopper beside him, he was the very picture of a contented yachtsman enjoying the sun, glad to be where he was and only waiting for her departure to allow him to fetch his supplies and have his breakfast. Sure enough, he stood up with a businesslike air.

'Give me that bag.'

'I'll manage...'

The wretched, tormenting hope washed through her again as he took the bag. But he only dumped it by the rail, clearly with nothing in mind except to speed her to the deck and out of his way. She scrambled out, doing her best not to touch him, but she needn't have bothered. As far as he was concerned, she might as well not have been there at all. Already he was sliding the cabin hatch into place with his back to her.

The sooner she was out of here, the better. Hardly knowing what she was doing, she climbed to the rail, shouldered the heavy bag, and manoeuvred herself over as best she could. Now it only remained to jump down to the pontoon. Here she went . . .

Only somehow, as she dropped the wretched bag, it caught and held, tangled in the rail. She was conscious of a horrible wrench in her shoulder and then the wooden planks of the pontoon came up to hit her.

CHAPTER NINE

DR CHARLOT fitted the X-ray photographs into place, switched the light on behind them, and studied them carefully.

'Ze bones,' his Gallic gesture soothed and stroked the air, 'are not damaged.'

Gemma gave her head a small shake to throw off her black, engulfing misery, and winced as the pain in her shoulder flared. 'Nothing's broken, then?'

'Not broken, not . . .'ow you say zees word?' His big Norman features creased with concentration. 'Not . . . dees-lo-ca-ted.'

'Th-thank you,' she murmured, and meant it.

She was sincerely grateful to this friendly little man for speaking to her in English. Nobody in Outpatients had known any, nor in the X-ray department—she couldn't have managed if it hadn't been for Bart's grasp of what was needed and his vigorously inventive sign language.

But then, she couldn't have managed without Bart at all. How on earth had he conjured up that wheelchair while she lay on the pontoon, dazed with humiliation and pain? She couldn't remember his asking for it—he'd seemed fully taken up wrapping wet cloths round her ankle—but he'd lifted her into it at once, as though he'd been expecting it, and whizzed her out to the taxi he had also seemed to be expecting, and held her steady all through the horrible drive to the hospital, just as if they hadn't parted for ever.

She'd even allowed herself to hope for a moment that she was wrong about that. But he hadn't changed his mind, she was only fooling herself. He'd not spoken a word to her. On their arrival in the hospital grounds he'd put her again in the wheelchair, and once she was safely with a nurse who understood what had happened, she'd seen no more of him.

And who could blame him? If a break had to be made, best to get it over quickly. Thanks to her stupid accident, he'd been forced to spend a beautiful morning looking after her, kicking his heels in dreary waiting-rooms, using his enterprise and his know-how to help her obtain the treatment she needed. And he'd done it all so patiently, so gently, only talking when something needed explaining, but always there to give her the help and protection she needed. Was it surprising if he'd had enough, and gone his own way? They were nothing to each other now.

'*Naturellement*, no standing, no walking,' the doctor was continuing. 'But in two weeks, you . . . 'ow you say? . . . you mend.'

'Th-thank you,' Gemma murmured again.

Pride forbade her to ask what she should do next. One way and another she'd caused enough trouble today for sensible people who had more important things to think about.

Only she did wish her tired, pain-weakened mind would start working again. How would she take this fortnight's rest? Where should she begin?

Perhaps with a taxi to the ferry? She'd need help on board, a taxi at the other end, more help... Her head started to swim, and she tried another tack.

Supposing she stayed here. That would mean wrestling with the language, finding a hotel, using her credit cards to draw French money...and where *were* her credit cards? Looking about her, she realised with despair that she didn't even have the wretched bag which had caused all the trouble.

The strongly built, rosy-cheeked nurse had returned, and Dr Charlot was speaking to her in his fruity-sounding French. He returned to English for Gemma.

'For ze shouldaire we 'ave a sleeng, for ze ankle a *bandage élastique*,' he explained, 'and zen you rest, rest, rest. 'e take care of you, your 'usband...'

'He's not...'

Gemma bit off the denial to thank him once more as he shook hands with her, then greeted the nurse in stumbling French. But while she was wheeled along endless corridors to a room lined with cupboards and drawers, she had no defence against the misery that was sweeping over her anew.

Her husband! If only he were.

But what's the good of thinking like that after he's gone? she scolded herself as the elastic bandage was fitted.

Gone because she'd been so sure she could manage on her own. And look at her, wasn't she managing well?

The sling was black, as if specially chosen to match her mood. She ducked her head to let it be fitted round her neck and, in spite of the relief as her arm relaxed into it, found she was blinking back tears. They were only weakness, she told herself fiercely, weakness and the shock of the fall.

He'd been courting her. A real old-fashioned courtship, like they had at home. And during that courtship he hadn't been afraid to tell her he loved her. He had held off for a while when she'd tried to put on her stupid act, but as soon as it had crumbled he had pledged himself to her quickly and openly, with a courage and generosity she herself could never have shown. No wonder he'd accused her so angrily of never having committed herself to him at all. Compared with him, she hadn't known the meaning of the word commitment.

But this wouldn't do, she was idealising him because he'd gone. She must remember instead how he'd spat out the words 'career woman', showing once more the depth of his prejudices. He'd have tried to change her just as Kevin had, and been all the harder to resist because he was so much stronger. Hadn't he divorced his first wife because of her career?

But, in spite of her misery and her anger, she couldn't let that pass. Even now, when she was trying to persuade herself she was well rid of him, she had to admit she didn't know why his marriage had broken up, only that it had hurt him badly. Why had it hurt him so much? Useless to wonder about that now, when it would never do her any good.

'*Voilà.*' The nurse was now taking command of the chair again, and was wheeling it along more endless corridors.

It was hateful to be so completely helpless. Even if she could have asked where they were going, she wouldn't have understood the answer. She simply had to sit still and let it happen, let herself be pushed to a wide reception area full of people she couldn't see because she only came up to their waists, because they were going all blurry, because of her weakness and the shock of the fall...

'Thank you very much.' A deep, marvellously familiar voice spoke above her head, presumably to the nurse. 'Here, what's all this?' It was on her level now, and a big handkerchief smelling of outdoors was mopping her eyes. 'The worst's over.'

'I'm not crying.' Fighting to keep her voice from choking, she heard it come out hard and toneless. 'May I have this?' She grabbed the handkerchief. 'I think I may be starting a cold...'

'Very likely.'

The voice had cooled, but then it would, wouldn't it? She struggled to put her thoughts in order, and summoned all her pride to face his contempt. She must be strong. He'd be leaving her soon and he mustn't guess how she was going to miss him—that, at least, she could spare herself.

'Right,' he snapped. 'Here we go, then.'

She stuffed the handkerchief in her pocket, ready to take control of her own affairs again. 'Could you just leave me at that hotel you mentioned...'

'Don't be silly.'

It was so much what she wanted to hear that she turned, careful of her right shoulder, to squint up at him over her left. Her foreshortened view showed him with chin set, mouth held in, prominent eyebrows level over the great Cornish nose and the hard grey eyes.

Well, thank heaven he intended to help her, but it was a good thing he'd become so unyielding, she told herself. She couldn't have borne it if he'd been kind again.

'The doctor says I have to rest,' she explained, 'And you must be wanting to get back to the *Felicity*.'

'I've fixed all that.'

'What do you mean?'

'Bill Varco's coming over from the boatyard to demonstrate it to M. Dumont. Then he'll sail it back.'

'You mean . . . you're leaving it?' Her voice rose in protest. 'You didn't need to do that!'

'How else am I to get you home?'

'Home . . .' Worn out with the effort of peering up at him, she slumped back in the chair.

So be it. She wouldn't need to find help on the ferry, Bart would help her. She didn't need to wonder how she would make the change from ferry to train, Bart would make it for her. He would take care of her all the way, and presently would bring her to her own land where she could make herself understood, to her own flat where she could rest and recover. It was going to be a lonely, bitter recovery, but at least she wouldn't have too many worries. Not too many, only one gigantic, overriding misery which she wasn't even going to look at just now.

Just now, and for a while yet, he'd be with her, even if she couldn't talk to him properly any more.

Even if she didn't see him he'd be there as he was now, guiding her through the hospital and into its parking area. Guiding her to this ambulance with the ramp for her wheelchair and the clamps to secure it within.

He finished fitting them, and looked at her without expression. 'All right?'

She nodded, tight-lipped.

'Won't be long now.' Clearly anxious to be rid of her, he slid into the seat next to the driver with a murmured instruction.

A grill on the dashboard produced a burst of crackly, incomprehensible speech. The driver answered before he set off, and exchanged further mysterious comments once they were on their way.

'Wait a minute.' Gemma peered out of the side window, trying to make sense of the uphill, increasingly countrified road. 'This can't be taking us to the docks.'

'Full marks,' Bart threw over his shoulder as they drew to a halt beside an empty field.

He opened his door, and no further questions were possible. The roar in the air, which until then she had accepted as just one more part of the general strangeness, assaulted her ears even more when he opened the double doors at the back to lower her to the road. The giant clattering hum cut them off from each other while he wheeled her across soft turf.

'A helicopter!' she gasped, unheard.

So that was why they'd been using an intercom. They must have been arranging a pick-up point where the noise wouldn't be too disturbing, and where an ambulance could park safely.

Gemma couldn't possibly have found the strength to turn back and shout up to Bart under those whirring blades. But directly beneath, where the noise was less, he left the handles of her chair and bent to her level with an easy doubling of his long legs.

'Is there anything you need before we start?'

'My bag . . .' she began.

He moved his arm and she saw the bag hanging from his shoulder, nearly touching the ground in his present crouching position.

'How did you organise this so quickly?' She was conscious of the shrillness of her own voice trying to be heard.

His deep tones dominated the machine-noise without effort. 'I do know a bit about organising.'

She shrugged, winced, and held her slung arm more carefully. It had been a silly question, anyway. Of course he knew about organising, that was one reason why he was rich. And, being rich, he could pay for what he wanted, pay to be rid of her as quickly as possible. For a man like him, time was money, the cost of a helicopter far less than the final cost of the hours he would have wasted on the longer crossing.

She mustn't feel this sinking in her heart. So they weren't going to be together much longer—that was neither here nor there. She must be grateful he was doing so much, more than she'd ever deserved, and forget that in a few hours she'd be alone in her wretched flat, knowing she'd never see him again.

Thank heaven she had another practical problem to cope with now. She looked up at the door of the cabin, trying to work out how she could climb through it without giving herself further pain. But even as she was unconsciously preparing her left arm and her right ankle to take the strain, Bart had risen to control her chair again, and the ambulance driver was wheeling a ramp over the turf. The ramp in place and adjusted, Bart pushed her up and brought her to rest as nearly as possible through the cabin door.

'Can you manage to get into that seat by yourself?'

'Of course.'

She scrambled awkwardly, favouring her right shoulder and her left ankle, from the wheelchair to the passenger seat. The one passenger seat—was he going to leave her already? And why was the pilot disappearing from his place?

She looked back to the meadow and found Bart shaking hands with the ambulance driver, the wheelchair already back on terra firma and handed over. As she watched, the helicopter pilot came into view again, and he too shook hands. Then Bart went round to the other side of the machine, out of her line of view for a moment, and climbed into the seat beside her. The door closed on them both, and she disguised her relief by fumbling with her belt, holding her breath as he leant towards her to help.

Help with her chair was one thing. It kept him at a distance, often not even in her line of vision. But this other help brought him much too close, and in spite of all they had been through, in spite of all the horrible things they had said to each other, his closeness disturbed her as much as ever.

'I'll manage.' She spoke too quickly and too shrilly.

He only clicked the buckle into place and sat back. 'Now, where do I take you?'

'You...you can pilot us?' She adjusted her voice, relieved to find the noise inside the machine was less of an exhausting, all-muffling blanket than it had been outside.

'They wouldn't have let me hire this if I couldn't. So,' he asked again with no sign of impatience, 'where to?'

'Well...London, I suppose.'

'You don't sound very sure.'

'I...' She looked round at the sunlit air, the blue sky, the cropped turf. 'I hadn't thought about it. Can you land absolutely anywhere?'

'Just about. They're handy things,' he went on, far better able to talk above the noise than she, 'you can put them down on cliffs, beaches, tiny little hills...'

She closed her eyes, not listening any more as she was swept into the vision his simple words had conjured up. The cliffs would be granite, surrounding and sheltering the sandy beaches in their bays and coves and inlets. The little hills would be green and sheep-dotted, with sudden views of the sea.

'Can we go home, please?' she asked, still with eyes shut.

So she missed the thrill of her first take-off in a helicopter, and didn't care. It was enough just to know Bart was in charge, guiding her away from everything that worried her, guiding her home. Home, to her mother's loving bossiness and her father's practical, unquestioning support; home, where Tamsin would bring the little ones in for a while, lively Jilly and quiet Patrick who had inherited his own father's steady good sense...

It was the noise stopping which woke her. The rattling roar had become so much a part of her world that its sudden absence brought her out of sleep as surely as an alarm clock.

'What's happened...where are we...'

She let him undo her seat-belt while she blinked round him through the perspex. In the distance a little harbour nestled between granite cliffs, its red-brown jetty reaching into a sea now turning violet in the lengthening rays of the sun. Nearer, the hillside blazed with gorse blossom and the hedge with campion.

'Why are we here?' she demanded, still half-asleep. 'I was going to tell you how to land in my parents' garden...'

'How lucky I didn't need your advice.'

Bristling at the cold irony, she woke fully. 'But Pensilva Haven, of all places!'

'It happens to be where my boatyard is.'

'Oh,' she muttered, cast down again. 'I'm sorry. I forgot.'

His craggy features warmed to a kindly, surprising smile, but it wasn't for her. He was waving, and she followed his gaze to a flash of bright red in the gateway a few yards off. A crop-headed young man was returning the wave with a broad grin as he left the little car and came towards them through the gorse. Bart opened his door and jumped down without further explanation, and Gemma watched in blank misery as he greeted the newcomer like an old friend, then quickly turned back to open her door.

'I'll help you down,' he told her, bleak as ever.

'I can manage . . .'

But she couldn't. She had shifted her weight too suddenly, and was forced to a halt by the stab in her shoulder.

'Slowly, now.' He reached up to put a hand each side of her knees. 'Start by getting yourself sideways.'

And his hands actually helped. Strung between the one pain in her shoulder and the other in her ankle, she concentrated on swivelling her slender hips until her knees were over the side of her seat, and the more those gentle hands lifted and pushed, the easier it became. She didn't have to let them remind her of pleasures lost for ever, any more than she had to think of them later when he took her up lightly in his arms.

The warmth of his body was there through the blue-green cloth of his jacket, but his eyes were granite-cold. She looked away from them and wondered when he'd found the time to change into his respectable shore-going clothes. Was there no end to the miracles of competence he could perform while she did nothing but hurt herself and make a mess of things?

'Come on, Bart.' The square young man spoke from somewhere by her. 'You keeping that all to yourself?'

'This,' Bart swung Gemma round to face their companion, 'is my future partner, Bill Varco.' His voice, which had softened for a moment, grew terse as ever. 'Bill, this is Gemma Roseveare, the . . . the person I'm helping.'

'You never mentioned her looks. If you had,' Bill Varco's spaniel eyes were alight, 'I'd have let you take the chopper back while I saw to the girl.'

'That'll be the day,' Bart grinned, 'when you turn down both a chopper to pilot and a yacht to sail, just for a girl.'

Gemma listened in mounting fury. To be described as 'the person I'm helping' was bad enough, but to be dismissed as not worth a chopper and a yacht! But in her present state, helpless as a child, she was quite unable to make any of the small gestures and cutting comments which would have put them both right. She could do nothing but seethe, and nod, and try to smile.

'Don't be so sure,' Bill Varco's eyes were lingering on her. 'If the girl's like yours . . .'

Gemma was aware of Bart's arms stiffening, of his muscles tensing in silent rejection of the idea that she was his girl. Then he turned away from Bill, and made a brief gesture with his head at the helicopter.

'You're quite clear on refuelling? And on where to land?'

'It's done, Chief.' Bill sketched a mock salute, businesslike at once. 'Mind how you set her at the hills, now,' he shouted back, already climbing into the machine.

'It's this he means, not you,' Bart carried Gemma to the red Volkswagen Beetle with 'Cindy' on its tail in curly gold lettering. 'He says she's a little good 'un when she's treated right.'

Gemma couldn't reply because the rotor blades whirred into life again. He lowered her to her feet and unlocked the passenger door, still holding her with one arm to support her on her good leg. The helicopter roared upwards and he gave it a farewell wave before helping her into the seat.

'Women and machines.' She belted herself in and leaned back on her headrest. 'You don't even know the difference.'

'Yes, I do. Machines are more reliable.'

I walked into that one, she thought, angry with herself, and changed the subject. 'How did he know you were coming?'

'I phoned him from Cherbourg, of course.'

'But that was before I asked to be brought here.'

'It was only a matter of changing the time by radio.' He had put the key in the engine and was buckling his own belt. 'I meant to come on here anyway, after I'd gone wherever I needed to drop you.'

'I'll be just as glad to be dropped as you'll be to drop me,' she hastened to assure him.

'Right, then we'll both soon be satisfied.' He started the engine and put it into gear. 'Your parents' address, please?'

She gave it.

'And you're sure they'll be there?'

'They always are.'

'Lucky you.' Easing them from the gateway to the road, he ground the words out as if he hated her. 'Though I bet you think that's thanks to your own cleverness...'

'I don't know what you're talking about.' She turned her head tiredly to look at him. 'What's lucky about having parents?'

'You're proving my point. And you've got *two* of them, always there.' He set the little car at the hill, grim-faced. 'Exactly half of which you expect to provide for your own son or daughter.'

She lolled back against the headrest, provoked again by his hostility. 'So we're back to that, are we?'

'Are you surprised? You're not fit to look after yourself, let alone a child.'

'Only now, it's none of your business,' she interrupted, and wished she could feel more satisfaction in that final, triumphant answer to all his criticisms of her. But she didn't, couldn't feel anything but blank misery.

'Twenty minutes from now, anyway.'

Reminded of how much help he had given her, she bit her lip. 'I know I've a lot to thank you for, Bart.'

'Mr Rule. And I don't want your thanks.'

'What do you want?'

'From you, nothing but...' he gave her a quick sideways glance '...what you'll never give me.'

'What's that?' she asked, suddenly breathless.

'The assurance you won't go any further with this half-witted scheme. That you won't collar another unfortunate man...'

'Poor thing, you're making me weep for him,' she burst out in a fury of disappointment.

'Weep for the baby.' He waited in a passing-place for a milk-tanker to go by. 'If you ever persuade a man to co-operate.'

'I'll let you know,' she said wildly, far too angry to tell him what she really felt now about the whole idea. 'I'll send you a postcard.'

He slowed down for a sharp corner. 'Make it a letter marked Private and Confidential,' he rapped out as he eased the accelerator down again. 'I'm particular about what my secretary reads.'

'She's a grown woman, isn't she?'

'Not that grown.'

'No woman is, according to you.'

'Let's get this straight here and now.' He scowled at the green tunnel of road, its high Cornish hedges foaming with wild flowers. 'You don't know anything about me, or about anybody, or about anything. And you never will.'

'And you, of course, do!'

'I know you're a smug little slogan-monger with a closed mind.'

'And you're a...a bad-tempered, unreasonable...'

'Male chauvinist pig,' he finished for her when she hesitated. 'I wonder where I've heard that before?'

'I—I wasn't going to say that,' she muttered, because it was the only put-down she could think of.

It was exactly what she had been going to say. But he was only getting the better of her because she was so tired, she told herself furiously. And, after all, she was an invalid—he shouldn't be arguing with her like this.

Determined not to let him provoke her again, she closed her mouth tight. Except for her brief instructions through the town, they drove the rest of the way in silence.

CHAPTER TEN

'POOR you.' Tamsin flopped her weight into the old spring rocker which had sat in the corner of Gemma's room as long as they could both remember. 'A cold now, on top of everything else.'

'Mum says it's *because* of everything else.' Gemma took another tissue from the packet and sneezed again. 'She says the accident shook me up, and let the germs in.'

'Did it start with a bit of a throat? Then a bit of a cough, and then this bit of sneezing?'

'I wouldn't call them *bits* of anything.'

'You must've got it worse than we all had, me and John and the kids.'

'I can see that.' Gemma looked enviously at her sister's clear eyes, the shining dark hair tucked back behind her ears, the glowing skin offset by a sleeveless shift of blue cotton.

What a contrast to her own reflection in the dressing-table mirror. The merciless June sun wasn't direct on her, but here in her white bedroom it might as well have been. Dim and red-rimmed as her eyes were, they spared her no detail of rat's-tail hair, pale cheeks and pink nose. She must have a mild temperature, too; she was shivering in spite of this enveloping cotton nightdress she'd borrowed from her mother.

'Would you tip that glass so I can't see into it?' she asked despondently. 'Being pregnant suits you better than this bug suits me.'

Tamsin leant forward to oblige. 'Mum let me come and see you because I've had it already.'

'I note she's kept the kids downstairs.'

'Well, she would, wouldn't she?' Tamsin smiled fondly at their mother's determined commandeering of her grandchildren. Then she turned to the open window, throwing back her head to take in the freshness of the garden and of the yellow roses climbing round the sash. 'Did you know your boyfriend's still here?'

'Don't call him my boyfriend,' Gemma ordered thickly through the tissue she had grabbed. She didn't need to sneeze again, but blew her nose noisily and hoped it would cover the knocking of her heart against her ribs.

This was exactly the encounter she'd been trying to avoid ever since her dramatic arrival here on Friday. Her parents, Tamsin, and even Tamsin's husband were still agog at the way Bart Rule had carried their Jen into the sitting-room, dumped her on the couch like a sack of potatoes, and refused to stay for a drink or a bite.

Knowing what a shock her sudden appearance like this would be, she'd made herself be polite to Bart until he went. But he hadn't responded, hadn't made the least attempt to conceal his distaste for her, only turned away from her with one of his kind, unexpected smiles for her parents.

Her mother had been completely won over by it. Her father might have been too, if the previous hostility to his daughter hadn't been so obvious. His children, right or wrong, Gemma thought with a rush of affection, that was Tom Roseveare's motto.

'I wouldn't talk about this outside, if I were you,' Bart had warned as he departed.

'We won't.' Gemma's father had reprimanded him with dignity.

And they hadn't. But that didn't stop each of them in their different ways trying to find out more than she was prepared to tell them.

She'd spent most of Saturday catching up on lost sleep, but it hadn't really helped much. She'd felt stronger by the end of the day but that had only sharpened her misery, and her irritation at having to fend off the family's curiosity. They'd each had their own way of showing it, her father in silent concern, her mother in open questioning, and Tamsin in sympathetic asides. Luckily, asides had been all Tamsin could manage until now. She'd have been the most difficult of all to fob off if it hadn't been for Patrick and Jilly's interruptions.

Gemma sighed; she might have known her sister would find a moment somehow, and she had. Sunday, which Tamsin always kept free to be with her husband and children alone, had come and gone, and they were back into the working week again. So now the children were downstairs being well taken care of by adoring grandparents, and here was Tamsin, free to use all her sympathetic insights and her inquisitive shrewdness to find out anything she could.

'I only stayed in bed because Mum made me,' Gemma snuffled. 'I wouldn't have, if I'd known you'd come up here and plague me about him.'

But she knew that was sheer bravado. She couldn't move much anyway on her damaged ankle, and with a cold as bad as this, bed was the only place for her. Once or twice in the sniffling quiet of her room she had realised how easily her sister could talk to her alone here, but each time she'd remembered Tamsin's pregnancy and relied on the bugs to keep her away. She had reckoned without Tamsin's serene good health having already conquered them.

The same serenity now kept her bouncing peacefully up and down in the rocker, ignoring the rebuff. 'I didn't mean he's right here in Fowey. He's staying at the Royal, in Pensilva.'

'Oh.' Gemma couldn't keep the flat disappointment out of her voice. 'That's because he's starting a business there.'

'He told me.'

Gemma stopped with the Vaseline half applied to her poor sore nose. 'You've talked to him?'

'Mum badgered Dad to write a thank-you note...'

'I bet Dad enjoyed that.'

'He did it in the end.' A fleeting dimple showed at the corner of Tamsin's mouth in loving amusement at the final surrender of her beleaguered father. 'But he wouldn't show us what he'd written. He put it straight in the envelope and sealed it.'

'Good for him.'

'Then Mum said I had to deliver it by hand.'

'And see what you could find out.'

'Don't be so sour, Jen. It doesn't suit you.'

'You've talked to him though, haven't you?'

'To Bart Rule?' Tamsin met her sister's eyes at last. 'Yes.'

'So he's told you,' Gemma said in resignation. She might have been angry if she'd had the energy, but she doubted it. Somehow nobody was ever angry with her sister, and anybody would tell her anything. Talking to her was like taking off a cloak in the sun.

'If you mean, about why you fell out,' Tamsin began carefully, 'how you'd been...' She met Gemma's eyes and gave up the attempt to be more explicit. 'What you'd been doing—yes, he told me that.'

'Tammy, if you let on to the folks, I'll murder you...'

'I'd never do that, Jen. I wouldn't want to hurt them.'

'No,' Gemma said soberly. Hurting her parents had been one of the many drawbacks of her plan to have a baby alone, a price she had decided must be paid. Now she was with them again, it seemed a more serious one than she had reckoned.

'I did my best to cheer him up. Said you could be silly...'

'Thank you, sister!'

'...but that you're decent enough at heart, and he mustn't think too badly of you.'

'With friends like you, who needs enemies?'

'Well, honestly, Jen!' Tamsin was as cross as she ever became, as cross as Jilly sometimes made her.

'Of all the idiotic ideas . . . and to ask Bart Rule, of all people.'

'Why not?' Gemma demanded, stung. 'He'd be a good father . . .'

Conscious of having already given away more than she meant to, she took another tissue and wiped all the Vaseline off her nose. Of course Bart would be a good father. He'd be even better as a husband for the lucky woman who finally got him. His first wife must have been mad . . .

'. . . must have been mad,' Tamsin was continuing. 'But there it was, she wanted the operation.'

'Who wanted what operation?' Gemma came out of her misery to find she'd been missing something she might really want to know. 'What are you on about?'

'Do listen to me, Jen! Mrs Rule . . .'

'D'you mean Caroline Lang?'

'If you like, but she *was* Mrs Rule, that's what matters . . .'

'It would be,' Gemma sniffed.

'Do you want to carry on with your London silliness, or will you listen?'

'Sorry,' Gemma apologised with a curtness that could barely have satisfied even her sweet-natured sister. 'What about Caroline Lang, then?'

'She didn't want children.'

'I thought she might not have.'

'So she asked to be sterilised.'

'Oh.' Gemma flopped back on her pillows, refusing to act as horrified as she felt. It was one thing not to want children—but to cut yourself off from the possibility of *ever* having them?' 'I . . . I can see it's a bit hard on him,' she admitted grudgingly.

'Bart Rule of all people!'

'Why do you keep saying "Bart Rule of all people"?' Gemma broke in, half-irritated and half-curious. 'What makes him so special?'

Tamsin stopped rocking, and stared out over the massive bulk of Number Three. 'D'you mean you can't see it?'

'See what?'

'How lonely he is, you twit!'

'Lonely?'

Gemma closed her eyes, trying to force her aching head to take it in. This was a completely new angle on the man who had meant so much to her for a week, and who in spite of everything still dominated her thoughts. On the millionaire employer who had friends everywhere, who—she admitted it—was nice enough to have friends even if he'd been poor.

'Lonely,' she repeated in wonder. 'I'd never thought...'

'With him, it's the first thing you *should* think,' Tamsin rocked again. 'His father dying so young, and his mother, too, when he was only fifteen.'

'I'd...sort of forgotten that,' Gemma muttered into the bedclothes.

The knowledge of her own stupidity had come to her like a blow, like the slap Bart had given her three days ago. As well he might, when she'd persisted with that stupid talk of why his wife had left him.

How could she? And how could she have failed for so long to pick up the signals her sister had understood in one brief talk? They'd all been there: the birthday present for his secretary's little girl, the pub where he ate with the family, his bitter reference to his flat as 'ideal for family occupation'— how ironic that must have seemed, to a man whose marriage had broken down over his wife's refusal to have children.

'Jilly's eating the soap, Mummy,' Patrick called up the stairs.

'Kids!' Tamsin rolled her eyes to heaven. 'Who'd have 'em?' She levered her weight out of the chair and paused at the door. 'Are you all right for aspirin and hot lemon and things?'

Gemma nodded, and turned to face the wall as the door closed softly.

Whenever she was ill, she only had to come home to be given every comfort her parents could provide. Their affection was all round her in hot-water bottle and thermos and flowers, the old teddy on her dressing-table, the drawers crammed with things she wouldn't have in her flat but wanted to keep.

Just like Bart wanted to keep the furniture which was all he had left of his parents. She thought of the hard city office with its old roll-top desk, its mahogany chairs and walnut table, its blue-sprigged china, and felt a new smarting of her eyes which had nothing to do with her cold. Tamsin would have seen the significance of that old furniture at once, but then Tamsin had never cut herself off from all the loving entanglements of family life.

And neither had Gemma, not really. She'd liked to think of herself as a loner because it sounded interesting, but she'd never really been one, never been more than first a spoilt little girl and then a woman growing set in her ways. 'A skinny old maid'... Bart's painful phrase came back to haunt her.

And 'grabbing everything you want like a monkey'. Trying to grab a pregnancy, a child, for no better reason than that she wanted one. Quite sure she could cope and not have to give up any of the other things she also wanted: her job, her freedom, her independence. Never once considering what that would all mean to the baby, let alone to the man she'd foolishly intended would help her conceive it.

She closed her eyes but there was no shutting out what she'd done. She'd coveted his warmth and his strength, but on her terms only. And so she had asked a man who had hardly known his own father to father a child who would hardly know him.

No wonder he'd been so grim when he'd met her parents! Their immediate, absorbed concern for her must have been the last straw, must have shown him so clearly how she'd always been able to take family warmth and care for granted. No wonder he'd gone his way, thankful to be rid of her, ready to meet somebody better.

He'd be sure to meet somebody better. Anybody was better than a woman who went on board a boat named *Happiness*, a family boat, with no intention but a brief coupling for her own selfish ends. Who had decided to have nothing more than a miserable half-family, with him on the outside where he'd always been.

No, if there was anything Bart Rule didn't need, it was a woman like her. One of these days she'd hear about the lucky one he finally chose, read it in the papers or be told by her family—that word again. And she'd think, *it could have been me*, and go on thinking it all the blank years of her life. All the years she had to live knowing she had thrown away her chance of happiness with the man she truly loved, knowing she had made him hate her for her thoughtless selfishness and her lack of imagination.

The tissue box was nearly empty, the bag where she kept used ones nearly full. She wished she felt strong enough to hobble down and burn it in the Aga, but her mother would be cross if she even tried. Besides, they'd all guess it wasn't her cold making her eyes so red and swollen, and they were worried enough about her already...

What was that? She sat up, painfully wrenching her shoulder while the sling dangled useless round her neck, and listened to the unmistakable noise of a big man moving lightly, a man taking the stairs three at a time.

'Bart!'

She couldn't keep the joy out of her voice, but it faded as she took in his appearance. Cold-eyed, tight-lipped, he clearly hadn't come to wish her well. In fact, he looked so angry that she wondered how he'd persuaded her parents to let him up here at all. Her father, too, could be forceful in defence of his own—why had he allowed this disturbance of her sick-room? Then she realised she'd heard her father's voice several times from the garden—he'd be in his vegetable patch. And Bart would have no trouble in charming his way past her mother.

'I talked to your sister this morning,' he began abruptly.

'I heard,' she mumbled.

'It's a pity you're not more like her.'

'She's an interfering busybody.'

'She's fond of you. For that matter, so's your Dad—I can't blame him really...'

'Blame him? What for?'

'You'd better read this,' he held out an envelope addressed in her father's clear, square script, 'BY HAND' printed in the corner where the stamp should have been. 'She said it was a thank-you note—that's why I've only just read it.'

Gemma read the letter first in amazement, and then in a fury which threatened to match his.

Dear Mr Rule,

    This is just to tell you what I think of the way you have treated our Jen. She is a good girl, even if a bit headstrong, and now she is moping about like a sick cat, we can't get any sense out of her at all, it is enough to make you weep the way she is pining. You take her on holiday and bring her home hurt, and all you can do is push off to your own affairs and enjoyments. But I hope some day your conscience will remind you of the unhappiness you have brought to a poor young girl.

                    Yours sincerely,
                    Thomas Roseveare

'I'll kill him!' Gemma flung back the sheet and staggered upright. 'Can you reach my dressing-gown off the door?' She sank to the bed again, brought down by weakness and the pain in her ankle and shoulder.

'Back to bed, you idiot.' He picked her up by the waist and dumped her against the pillows. Still with his hands on either side of her waist, he sat back and surveyed her. 'If this is the way you've been looking, I'm not surprised he's worried.'

'That's right.' She shook her straggly hair out of her eyes. 'Rub it in.'

'What have you been doing to yourself?'

'I'll tell you what I haven't been doing, and that's pining.'

'You could have fooled me.'

'You're all alike, you men, think we can't live without you.' '"Sick cat", indeed,' she quoted through gritted teeth. '"Poor young girl", indeed!'

'It's only because he loves you. I'd do the same for my own daughter.'

'Not if she was mine too, you wouldn't.'

Gradually, almost too slowly for it to be noticeable at any individual moment, his expression had been softening, his eyes almost dancing. Now they hardened abruptly.

'Why did you let him think it was all my fault? Why didn't you tell him the truth?'

For a moment she stared back, pinned by his hands against the pillows. Then she turned her head away. 'I'm going to sneeze.'

'No, you're not.'

But as he spoke one of his hands had left her waist and gone to the back pocket of his jeans. She was cold without that hand on her waist, but she could bear it for the sake of the handkerchief he gave her. It was so much nicer than tissues for mopping your tears, a handkerchief that smelt of outdoors. Just as his shoulder in the creamy, knobbly Aran sweater was nicer to cry on than a hot, crumpled pillow.

'You'd...b-better leave it here to...b-be washed,' she wept, trying to calm herself by thinking of practical matters. 'With th-that other one you l-lent me...'

'If you're going to do much of this,' he smoothed the hair back from her hot forehead, 'I'll have to lay in a new supply.'

'Be careful. You'll catch my cold.'

'Why not? I seem to have caught you...'

'You haven't,' she sobbed crossly. 'That is, you c-can't even... w-want me...'

He cupped her face in his hands, holding it still and forcing her to look into his eyes. 'Will you ever tell your dad why I was so angry with you?'

She tried to look down, but he wouldn't let her. All she could do was to drop her eyelids, giving herself a double view of her shining pink nose.

'Will you?' he demanded implacably.

She felt her cheeks press against first one of his hands, then the other, as she tried to shake her head.

'And why not?'

'B-because...' She sniffled, and applied the handkerchief. 'Because it would make him ashamed of me.'

'And why would it do that?'

'Because he thinks it's wrong to have babies out of wedlock.'

'And you still don't?'

'N-not exactly.'

'So why are you crying?'

'C-can I blow my nose, please?'

He released her, and she flopped back on the pillows with the handkerchief to her nose. She felt chilled without his touch on her face, but his weight was still beside her on the bed, pressing her thigh. When she had mopped her eyes again, and taken a deep, uneven breath, she thought she could say what she must.

'I'm s-sorry, Bart.'

'I should think so, too.' He went on, relentless as ever, 'Now say what you're sorry for.'

'It . . . it'll take a long time.'

'I have the time.'

'Have you, Bart?' She looked at him wonderingly. 'Have you really any time for me at all, after the way I've behaved?'

'Let's just say, with a nice, sensible family like yours . . .'

'So it's only my family you like?'

'I wouldn't say that.' His eyes lingered on hers. 'You're . . . you're a very good crew for the *Felicity*.'

'My family and my crewing. But what about *me*?' She regarded him anxiously. 'What's there about *me* for anybody to want, Bart?'

'I can think of a thing or two.'

'Enough to be worth marrying me?'

'Enough to consider it, certainly.'

'I'd give up my job,' she promised eagerly, 'as soon as the baby came...'

'I'd never ask you to do that. After all,' he put one hand on her hip, light and comforting through the bedclothes, 'I'd be there to help.'

'We'll have to be quick, you see,' she explained through a final hiccuping sob.

'In case he's already on the way, you mean?'

'That, too. But if he isn't, we have to keep trying, haven't we? I'm not getting any younger.'

'Oh, my darling!'

'Careful, you'll catch my cold...'

'Why not?' he said again before his lips met hers in a light, tender kiss which made no demands. 'What's yours is mine now.'

'How do you set about getting a special licence?'

She stopped as the bedroom door swung slowly inward. At first she thought it was opening itself, moved perhaps by the sheer weight of family concern on the other side of it. However, she quickly realised she had been looking for the intruder in the wrong place.

Or rather, at the wrong level. From knee-height, Jilly regarded them, wide-eyed.

'She's just as nosy as the rest of my family,' Gemma told Bart, 'and naughty enough to follow you up.'

Bart left the bed to pick the little girl up and cuddle her, but wasn't allowed to hold her for long. Quick, feminine footsteps mounted the stairs, and Gemma's mother appeared in pursuit.

'I'm so sorry.' She held her arms out commandingly for her grand-daughter. 'She's got a will of her own, this one.'

'Like her aunt,' Bart murmured.

'Her aunt?' Mrs Roseveare left off smoothing Jilly's hair to work it out. 'Oh—you mean our Jen?'

'So you really do call her Jen?' Bart asked, mouth quirking, 'It's not the name I'm used to.'

'Oh, that's just her London nonsense, Mr Rule.'

'Bart.'

'Bart,' Mrs Roseveare repeated, blue eyes sparkling. 'We're just going to have lunch... Bart. There'd be enough...'

'Thanks, I'd have loved it.' He looked as if he meant it. 'But I've already eaten.'

'Coffee, then?'

'Great! And if you don't mind,' he added, 'I'll just stay here and keep company with... with your Jen.'

'Are you really going to call me that?' Gemma demanded as her mother bustled away.

'I certainly am.' He seated himself again at her side. 'And so is everybody else, from now on.'

'I called myself Gemma specially for London.'

'And now you're done with it.'

'Well, all right.' She pretended to consider. 'But if I give it up, will you stop wearing those awful old clothes?'

'My sailing gear, you mean?' he asked in mock outrage.

'Especially the cap.'

'My cap? Certainly not. But don't worry,' he gave her a wicked grin, 'for our honeymoon on the

Felicity, I won't be wearing clothes much at all, will I?'

'Oh, Bart!'

She remembered her blissful days on the boat named *Happiness*. The thought of more like that, of a whole lifetime like that, was enough to make her sneeze again. She held it back, trying to keep to her role of hard bargainer. 'Well, all right. But you have to dress respectably when we go ashore.'

'For you, anything.'

'I'll believe that when I see it.'

She managed to get it out, and then the sneeze wouldn't be held back any longer. She let it rip.

'So that's settled then, our Jen.'

'Whatever you say, Bart.'

'And I'll believe that when I see it. He repeated her words with a grin. 'Still, we might as well try it.'

He considered taking both her hands. But her right one was still clutching his handkerchief, so he contented himself with picking up her left.

'Now, then,' he enclosed the third finger in his gentle grip, 'say after me, "I, Jennifer Roseveare, take thee, Hobart Rule..."'

COMING IN JUNE

THE MASTER FIDDLER

Jacqui didn't want to go back to college, and she didn't
want to go home. Tombstone, Arizona, wasn't in her
plans, either, until she found herself stuck there en route
to L.A. after ramming her car into rancher Choya Barnett's
Jeep. Things got worse when she lost her wallet and
couldn't pay for the repairs. The mechanic wasn't
interested when she practically propositioned him to get
her car back—but Choya was. He took care of her bills and
then waited for the debt to be paid with the only thing
Jacqui had to offer—her virtue.

Watch for this bestselling Janet Dailey favorite, coming in
June from Harlequin.

Also watch for *Something Extra* in August and *Sweet
Promise* in October.

JAN-MAS-1

ANNOUNCING . . .

The Lost Moon Flower
by Bethany Campbell

Look for it this August
wherever Harlequins are sold

HR 3000-1

You'll flip . . . your pages won't!
Read paperbacks *hands-free* with

Book Mate • I

The perfect "mate" for all your romance paperbacks
Traveling • Vacationing • At Work • In Bed • Studying
• Cooking • Eating

Perfect size for all standard paperbacks, this wonderful invention makes reading a pure pleasure! Ingenious design holds paperback books OPEN and FLAT so even wind can't ruffle pages — leaves your hands free to do other things. Reinforced, wipe-clean vinyl-covered holder flexes to let you turn pages without undoing the strap . . . supports paperbacks so well, they have the strength of hardcovers!

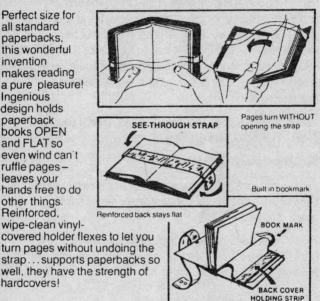

Pages turn WITHOUT opening the strap

SEE-THROUGH STRAP

Reinforced back stays flat

Built in bookmark

BOOK MARK

BACK COVER HOLDING STRIP

10 x 7¼ opened
Snaps closed for easy carrying, too

Available now. Send your name, address, and zip code, along with a check or money order for just $5.95 + .75¢ for postage & handling (for a total of $6.70) payable to Reader Service to:

Reader Service
Bookmate Offer
901 Fuhrmann Blvd.
P.O. Box 1396
Buffalo, N.Y. 14269-1396

Offer not available in Canada
* New York and Iowa residents add appropriate sales tax.

BM-G

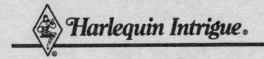

They went in through the terrace door. The house was dark, most of the servants were down at the circus, and only Nelbert's hired security guards were in sight. It was child's play for Blackheart to move past them, the work of two seconds to go through the solid lock on the terrace door. And then they were creeping through the darkened house, up the long curving stairs, Ferris fully as noiseless as the more experienced Blackheart.

They stopped on the second floor landing. "What if they have guns?" Ferris mouthed silently.

Blackheart shrugged. "Then duck."

"How reassuring," she responded. Footsteps directly above them signaled that the thieves were on the move, and so should they be.

For more romance, suspense and adventure, read Harlequin Intrigue. Two exciting titles each month, available wherever Harlequin Books are sold.

INTA-1